The PASSING *of the* GIBBOUS MOON

The PASSING of the GIBBOUS MOON

LARRY TURNER

The Passing of the Gibbous Moon

Copyright © 2020 by Larry Turner. All rights reserved.

No part of this publication may be reproduced, stored in a retrieval system or transmitted in any way by any means, electronic, mechanical, photocopy, recording or otherwise without the prior permission of the author except as provided by USA copyright law.

This novel is a work of fiction. Names, descriptions, entities, and incidents included in the story are products of the author's imagination. Any resemblance to actual persons, events, and entities is entirely coincidental.

The opinions expressed by the author are not necessarily those of URLink Print and Media.

1603 Capitol Ave., Suite 310 Cheyenne, Wyoming USA 82001
1-888-980-6523 | admin@urlinkpublishing.com

URLink Print and Media is committed to excellence in the publishing industry.

Book design copyright © 2020 by URLink Print and Media. All rights reserved.

Published in the United States of America
Library of Congress Control Number: 2020906453
ISBN 978-1-64753-315-1 (Paperback)
ISBN 978-1-64753-316-8 (Digital)

16.03.20

The football game for the Wills Wildcats was to determine the district championship. This November Friday night in 1998 was the first time the school had a chance to be district champs in seventeen years. As the game approached the final seconds, it was obvious the game was going to be determined in a last second climax.

JACKET FOREWORD
by East Texas writer, Buz Craft

Life was coming mighty fast for 17-year-old Todd Perry. The six-foot-three-inch athlete had just quarterbacked the Wills Wildcats to a district championship—but before he could really celebrate, his relationship with Denise Pool would become an adventure! Then, almost as unexpected, he was to kiss the tender lips of the girl of his dreams! Later, Todd is pressed to his limits in trying to protect himself and the injured Denise from the freezing elements—and ferocious wild animals—while lost in a vast, trackless forest. The question becomes, how will Todd react to these bizarre twists and turns; how will he stack up?

Author Larry Turner, an accomplished teacher and high school coach himself, delicately assembles here the trials, the tribulations and the triumphs of this young man who portrays the typical youth of today. The writer, however, does not fail to recognize and duly note the atypical circumstances that each individual must ultimately face.

This writer skillfully lays it out in an easy to read and non-didactic way: These are the pitfalls Todd faces, these are the choices he makes, and these are the results. This book is a must-read for all teenagers; and as it vividly portrays the world our youths inhabit—it likewise serves as a handy guide for older readers who truly want to see these youngsters reach their grandest potentials.

Dedicated to:
My wife Theresa, my best friend.

My daughter, Wendi Prescott, a very special person to everyone she meets.

Son in law, Byron, who loves to travel.

My son, Len, a lover of sports and successful tennis coach.

Daughter in law, Angel dedicated wife and mother.

Granddaughters, Hope, Kayla, and Taylor, adding joy to life.

Grandson, Lance, lover of sports, and a friend to everyone.

In loving memory of my parents, Preston and Alice Ruth Turner.

My brother Ron, a dedicated husband and father.

It is with special appreciation to several people that I acknowledge my gratitude for making this book possible.

To my wife Theresa for being my first reader and best critic.

To Elizabeth Rinks for correcting so many English errors.

To Dr. William Atkinson for medical advice, and Attorney Richard Currin for his legal suggestions.

To Elizabeth Miracle McBride for helping me clear up certain ideas.

To my brother Ron Turner for helping fly a rescue mission.

To many of my high school students and all of the teachers who read the manuscript and encouraged me to finish this project.

CHAPTER 1

Todd watched as Danny hit the line with a big thud! *"Man! He didn't make it,"* Todd thought as the whistles blew. Now it was fourth down and one at the one yard line, and the clock was running with twenty-seven seconds to go. The scoreboard read Big Town 13, Wills 7; the whole football game was going to rest on the last play of the game.

This was a cool November night, and the district championship was sitting on the one yard line. The town of Wills hadn't won a district championship in seventeen years. This play was going to be their last chance.

Everyone jumped and yelled as Coach Berry sent in the final play. Todd hollered at Stanley, "Hurry up!"

Stanley ran up to Todd and said, "Pro right, option left."

Todd was stunned. *"Option left?"* He thought. *"Why option left? Coach knows that I'm right handed, and the option to the left is much harder. The championship is on the line, and time is running out!"*

Todd sprinted to the huddle and called, "Pro right, Option left, on one…Pro right, Option left, on one." As the team sprinted to the line of scrimmage, Todd shouted, "Hurry!"

The fans were all standing, the bands were playing, and the excitement of Friday night football in a small Texas town was at its highest. On the home sideline, the cheerleaders were standing as close to the field as they could. No one had noticed that, as the drama was reaching a climax, there was no organized cheering taking place.

Everyone was caught up in the moment. Denise Poole, one of the local cheerleaders, was standing on the sideline with her hands clasped over her mouth and was jumping up and down in a nervous motion. Quietly she said to herself, "*Come on Todd; make it work.*"

She only knew Todd as a classmate. For some reason the starting quarterback didn't mix with many of his classmates, but at this moment, the game was in his hands.

As the six-foot-three-inch quarterback sprinted to the ball, he noticed that in the confusion of the last play, the split left end, Stanley Wilson, was left uncovered. He was wide open!

Todd quickly checked off to a quick slant-in pass. "Blue in, Blue in," the excited quarterback hollered. He instantly called, "Down...Set...Hut one!"

Todd took the football and started down the line to his left, just like the option, but instead of running the option to the left, Todd raised his arm to throw. Just as he was releasing the ball, he was hit by a hard-charging defensive lineman. The ball wobbled badly to the slanting split end. Stanley dropped to his knees and cradled the football just inside the end zone for the tying score.

As Todd was getting up, the extra point team was running onto the field; some of them were jumping with excitement. Todd was so relieved that the check off play had worked that he found himself jumping in the air. He didn't remember doing that very many times, but this was a big moment; and he felt that he owed it to himself to get a little excited. Besides, what was Coach Berry going to say to him when he got to the sideline?

Right now, they had to make the extra point. Fortunately, Todd was responsible for holding the ball for the kicker on this team. That would buy him a little more time before he would have to face his coach.

"Kick on hands, kick on hands," Todd repeated as they broke the huddle.

The team broke the huddle for the possible game winning point. There were only three seconds showing on the game clock. Todd sure didn't want a tie; that was like kissing your sister. He didn't have a sister, but he didn't think that would be any fun. A tie game wasn't acceptable.

The home team got to the line of scrimmage and lined up for the extra point. Todd made sure that everyone was down and set before he raised his hands for the snap. When he flicked his hand, he knew the ball would be there quickly.

When everyone was set, he gave the signal, and zip, the ball was there. From that point forward, everything would be automatic. Before Todd realized what was going on, the football was kicked into the air and through the uprights.

The noise level was louder than he could remember. Everyone was jumping around like children. This was beyond comprehension. With three seconds on the clock, Wills was ahead 14 to 13.

During all of the excitement, Todd realized that he was moving to the sideline and Coach Berry. There he was right in front of him, and he appeared to be satisfied at the moment. As Todd reached the side of the field, Coach Berry stuck out his hand and said, "Nice call, Todd."

As Todd went by the coach, he felt the big pat on the butt that coaches always seem to do. Todd was glad to know that the coach had approved of his change of plays. At least he thought that the coach approved.

Todd took off his helmet and watched Coach Berry and Coach Mike Rhodes as they huddled the kickoff team on the sideline. While the manager gave him a cup of water, Todd watched as the coaches sent the team onto the field.

"Just get the ball in play, and keep it on the ground," Coach Rhodes hollered.

Coach Berry shouted to his kickoff team, "Cover and don't let anyone through!!"

As the kicker approached the ball, the whole stadium seemed to maintain an eerie silence. The ball fluttered on the ground as it rolled the necessary ten yards to be legal; then there was a massive scramble for the ball as the clock ran out! That was it! District champions! Wow! What a feeling as everyone on the sideline began to hug each other.

Both teams, soiled from dirty combat, moved to the middle of the field to congratulate each other for an exceptional game. Everyone had played extremely hard to be the champion.

As Todd approached the middle of the field, he passed Denise.

"Nice game, Todd," Denise said.

"Thanks!"

He had never paid much attention to girls, but there was something different tonight. For some reason, he looked back at her. *"Hmmm, nice legs,"* Todd thought. *"Why haven't I noticed her before?"*

The football team huddled in the middle of the field to have a prayer like they always did after a game. Tonight, there were a lot more people on the field. Many were parents and friends of the players, as well as many classmates.

Coach Berry told everyone that they had accomplished more than just a championship.

"Tonight," he said, "you have brought a community together for a common goal, a district championship. Tonight we were all one." As emotion filled the coach, he continued, "In two weeks we are going to take this community to a new level. We will be playing the first bi-district game in seventeen years."

Everyone yelled in approval at the coach's statement, but everyone got quiet as the he knelt to pray. As the players took off their helmets, Coach Berry prayed, "Father, thank you for the honor of being real champions. Help us to be Your champions every day. Amen!"

The players and fans immediately jumped up and started celebrating again.

Todd started off the field, but he glanced toward the visitors as they were leaving the field. Most of them had their heads down, some were wiping tears from their eyes, but all of them knew that they had played their hardest. They had come within three seconds—just one play—of being champs.

The district champions were leaving on the opposite side of the field. Todd noticed several fathers walking off the field with their arms around their sons.

He had lived with his grandfather, Poppy, for the past two years. His parents had been killed in an airplane crash about eight years earlier, and since that time he had lived with aunts and uncles on his mother's side. Todd had moved in with Poppy, his dad's father, to finish his last two years of high school.

Poppy had been good to him, but he was now in his late seventies and couldn't do many things that a teenager would enjoy doing. However, Poppy didn't miss any home games and would always be at the gate leaving the field when Todd would get there. Poppy would always say, "Nice game, son."

Several people came by to congratulate Todd on his game-winning touchdown pass, and those comments made him feel good. He was trying to take in all of the excitement and feelings that he could. He wanted to remember this moment forever. He thought, *"Man! What a feeling!"*

Denise was leaving the field with her date, Darren Hornsby, a rich college sophomore who always dressed in the most expensive clothes.

As they left the field, Todd noticed the couple and how Darren had put his arm around her waist with the attitude that he owned her. Todd wondered why this caught his attention tonight. He just knew Denise as a classmate and had never really paid much attention to what she did. Maybe it was just that Hornsby guy. Todd didn't care for Darren's type, anyway.

Denise went to put her megaphone and pom poms in Darren's car and told him that she was going to the front of the field house to see the players as they left the stadium. Darren tried to discourage her from going to the front. "Why do you always feel like you have to see everyone when they leave?" Darren fumed. "You just talked to them on the field," he complained.

Denise snapped back, "I'm a cheerleader, and it's part of my responsibility to do as much as I can to encourage the players!"

The two argued back and forth as they continued to the front of the field house. Darren tried to get Denise to skip out tonight, but she continued to refuse.

In the dressing room, Coach Willie gave all kinds of orders.

"Okay guys, pants in a stack, game jerseys in a stack, and game socks in a stack. If there are any injuries, be sure to get them checked before you leave tonight!"

By now most of the players were walking around naked, as most were either going in or coming out of the shower. Coach Berry hollered, "Watch the slick floor; we don't need anyone hurt taking a shower!"

Todd guessed that coaches always worried about things like that. It's one thing to get hurt during a game, but to get hurt taking a shower would be on the embarrassing side.

Several fathers and classmates were in the dressing room enjoying the championship victory. The room usually cleared out fairly quickly after a game. Some of the players had dates, some were going to a party, and some were just going home. They had to be back for a short practice and video tape by ten o'clock Saturday morning. If they stayed out too late, it would be hard to get going in the morning.

Clay Comer asked Todd, "Hey Bud! Need a ride home?"

Todd knew that Clay always had a date after a home game and would be sure to have one after such a big game as they played tonight.

Todd promptly declined, "Thanks, Clay, maybe next time."

He only lived a few blocks from the field, and for some reason he had a strong desire to walk home tonight.

Several of the players had left the field house when Coach Berry called, "Todd!" The coach hesitated for a moment, "That was a very alert call at the line of scrimmage."

Todd smiled at the coach's statement.

"In the heat of battle," he continued, "a lot of high school quarterbacks would have never seen that open receiver."

"Thanks, Coach!" Todd beamed.

He then thought, "*Coach didn't say anything about that wounded duck pass I threw.*" Todd continued to wonder, "*Does he know that I really didn't want to run that option left.*" Maybe he should tell Coach that the situation on the one yard line was not the place to run the option to the left. "*Ah,*" Todd thought, "*I'll talk to him tomorrow. For now I'm going to enjoy tonight's victory.*"

Players were coming out of the dressing room fairly fast by now. Some were by themselves, and some were in groups. Many of the fans, classmates, and parents had gathered to cheer for them when they came out the door.

Todd was one that came out alone. The applause made him feel good all over. He tried to savor this moment. Winning was great. He remembered one of his coaches sayings, "*Winning isn't everything; it is the only thing!*" He smiled to himself as he thought about that statement.

When he strolled by Denise, they smiled at each other, but as he passed her, their eyes touched. Todd noticed for the first time how brown and deep they were. There was something about those brown eyes he had never noticed before.

He thought to himself, "*They kinda reach out and grab you.*"

He didn't linger, but continued to move through the mass of people, listening to the comments people were making about how well he had played tonight.

Todd pulled up his jacket as he left the excited crowd. He only lived a few blocks up the street, and he knew he would be home shortly. These cool fall nights were a welcomed relief from the hot games played earlier in the season.

He glanced up at the gibbous moon. On a clear, crisp night like tonight, you could see all of the spots on the moon, almost like it was being magnified.

The gibbous moon, about three-quarters full, always reminded Todd of a football. Tonight of all nights, it looked like someone had thrown a nice smooth spiral pass. With that thought, he remembered the wobbly pass that he had thrown to Stanley for the winning touchdown. "*Wow! What a feeling!*"

Todd turned serious as his thoughts wandered to his parents. Eight years earlier, his life had been full of love and happiness. His parents had taken care of all his needs. All of that had ended in a fiery plane crash as they were going to a convention in Chicago.

He thought, "*Boy! Was that a blow!*"

His life had been jolted into a nightmare. After living with his aunts and uncles for five years, he moved to Wills a little over two years ago to live with his grandfather, "Poppy." Poppy loved Todd and tried to meet his needs, but it just wasn't the same as having his parents.

As Todd glared at the snow-white moon, it looked smeared as tears formed in the corners of his eyes. *What would it have felt like to have Dad walk me off the field tonight?* He would have been excited, smiling from ear to ear. He would have had his arm on my pads talking about that "beautiful spiral pass" that Stanley caught for the game winner.

He wiped his eyes clear with the cuff of his jacket as he slowed the pace of his walk home. Todd could not remember a game that Mom and Dad had ever missed when he played little league baseball. How could their exciting trip turn so sour?

Poppy always made his home football games, but he would never come on the field after a game. That was all right because Todd knew that Poppy was self-conscious about his age. Being self-conscious didn't keep him from taking his spot at the gate, however; he would let the younger parents go on the field, but his, "Nice game, son" was always waiting for him at the end of the field.

Todd could now see the little shack around the corner. He thought, *"Why am I so melancholy tonight?"* His team had just won the championship game, and he had been the hero. He should be elated. He just wished that his parents could have shared in his victory tonight. They loved to watch him compete and would have cherished this great game.

It was hard to figure what his life would have been like had they not been killed in that crash. He thought about the things he would have had—a car, nice clothes, and probably a girlfriend.

His parents had left him a large trust fund from an insurance policy, but he wouldn't have access to that money until he turned eighteen. That was no help to him now.

Who knew how life would have been different had they lived? Of all the things he could think of, the thing he would have loved the most would have been his father's arm on his soiled shoulder pads tonight.

He entered the unkempt yard with junk scattered all around, thinking about the "What ifs." Todd was sure of one thing: they would have been proud, boasting parents tonight.

As he came to the broken, uneven sidewalk under the big oak tree, he paused and looked at the football-shaped moon. Did they know? Were they proud? Were they in Heaven watching him at this moment?

Looking up, he closed his teary eyes and visualized them, arms around each other, smiling at him. He thought he caught a glimpse of his father as he cast a thumbs up at him. That was how his father used to signal to Todd from a distance that he approved of what his son had done.

Todd opened the flimsy screen door, pushed open the solid, poorly-painted, wooden door and entered the cold, dark living room. During his walk home, he had had the feeling that he had shared tonight's game with his loving parents. He was glad that he had turned down Clay's offer to ride. These precious moments with his parents' memory was worth the walk.

Poppy would already be in bed by this time of the night, but Todd hadn't missed his, "Good game, son," when he had left the field. It was around 11:30, and Todd wasn't the least bit sleepy after such an exciting football game. He reached over to the old rustic lamp table and picked up the western thriller that he had been reading and eased into his favorite recliner.

These books always helped him relax. There was something about life in the Wild West that fascinated him. Sometimes those years seemed so simple, yet at times total survival was all that mattered. Todd could always put himself into these stories. He wasn't a "cowboy," but he enjoyed the thought of living in western times.

Before he started reading his novel, his mind slipped back to Denise. For a moment it seemed as though she was in the room with him. Todd said to himself, "*Man, I believe those eyes could hypnotize a guy. Can you imagine looking into those brown eyes up close?*"

He had known Denise since coming to Wills, but for some reason, he had never really paid any attention to her, or any other girl as far as that goes.

Todd suddenly snapped back to reality as the book he was holding began to slip from his grasp. *"Why am I thinking about girls all of a sudden?"* he thought.

Girls had never been that important to him before, so why was he thinking about them now. Maybe he could be starting to mature as a member of the male sex.

He slowly got up from his reclining chair, went to the refrigerator, and poured himself some Coke. Stiffness was slowly setting in from the contact sport that he had been playing. Returning to his recliner, he sipped on his Coke and put those puzzling thoughts of girls out of his mind. His thoughts slowly turned to his western novel and the ability to survive a winter in the Rocky Mountains.

· · · · · · · ● · · · · · · ·

Denise and Darren went to a party at the Walkers' house after leaving the football field. Several of their friends and classmates were there. The music was loud as it usually was at a party. People were scattered throughout the house, and some had ventured outside to the backyard.

The night was cool and crisp, but not exceptionally cold. Darren lead the way as he and his date ventured to the backyard and around the east corner of the house, where the moon was slowly reaching the top of the sky.

Darren put his arm around Denise and pulled her close. They had been kissing for several moments when his hands began to roam about Denise's sleek body. She took his hands in hers and calmly removed them from her breasts, but they just seemed to bounce right back where she didn't want them.

Pulling back, Denise firmly protested, "Stop it! What is with you tonight?"

Darren commented softly, "Don't you think that we have known each other long enough to be more...ah, say...personal?"

Denise snapped back, "I am not ready to make those kinds of commitments. I think we need to go back inside."

Her frustrated date wasn't about to give up so easily and began to force her to kiss him.

"Stop it!" Denise shouted, and she pushed him back.

Darren, refusing to give in, said, "Come on, you know you want to be with me."

Before Denise knew what she was doing, she had slapped Darren across the face with the palm of her hand. As he quickly let go, she ran into the house and went into a hall bathroom, where she locked the door. She could never remember slapping or hitting someone with that kind of force. She thought, "*That's scary!*"

She liked Darren, but on the other hand, she was a senior in high school and had plans to go to college next fall. She didn't want to have permanent commitments to Darren at this time.

She needed to get home! Denise and her mother had always had a good relationship, and at this moment she felt the need to talk to her about the situation. If anyone would understand her concern, her mother would be that person.

Denise thought she could hear Darren come in the house looking for her. She put the top of the commode down, sat on top of it, and put her pretty face in her hands. "*How embarrassing!*" she thought to herself.

She thought, "Some of my friends are sexually active, drink some, and take chances."

Denise was from a close family and hadn't gotten involved in things as many of her friends had.

Her father was a highly-respected district attorney, they attended church regularly, and she was active in her church's youth activities.

She wondered, *"How could I have let this happen tonight? Am I so naive that I didn't see it coming?"* Questions were beginning to fill her head.

"*Was that Darren leaving?*" she asked herself as she listened at the bathroom door. It sounded as if he had left the party upset after asking several people about Denise.

No one seemed to have seen her come into the house or knew where she was. She waited a few more minutes, which seemed an eternity, before she opened the door and looked out.

She didn't see Darren anyplace, so she sneaked into the den where several couples were dancing. When she ran into Mandi Stowe, one of the cheerleaders, Denise whispered, "Mandi, I need to talk to you for a moment."

The two attractive cheerleaders stepped outside, just past the sliding glass door. "What's wrong?" Mandi asked.

"I need a ride home," Denise said as she looked around to see if anyone was watching.

"Sure," Mandi answered, but there was a puzzled tone in her voice, as if she knew something had happened to her friend. "I need to let my date know that I will be back in a few minutes, and I will need to borrow his car," Mandi stated as she went back into the house to get her purse and some keys.

When they left the party, Mandi could tell that Denise was upset about something and asked if she could help.

Denise was now fighting back the tears, partly from her experience with Darren and partly from embarrassment. Denise simply told her friend that she had had a disagreement with Darren, and she thought he had left the party. All she wanted right now was to get home.

Wills being a small town, the Pooles' house was but a few minutes from the Walkers' house, so it didn't take Mandi long to get her friend home.

"Thanks for the ride," Denise told the other cheerleader. "I'll talk to you later," she continued as she got out of the sporty car.

"Good night, Denise. We had an exciting game tonight, and you need to enjoy it some," Mandi commented.

"I will!" Denise came back. "I'm okay."

As Mandi drove away from the Pooles' house, Denise took a deep breath and, for the first time since her nerve-racking experience with Darren, seemed to relax in the comfort of her own home.

It had been a great game tonight, and she had enjoyed the excitement and intensity of the whole evening, with the exception of what had happened at the party.

Denise opened the front door and entered the house, locking it as she closed it behind her. She knew that her mother would be awake; her parents never would go to sleep until their daughter was home, and she knew that would be the case tonight. Taking off her shoes, she slipped down the hall to her parent's bedroom.

Her mother calmly asked, "Have a good time tonight, dear?" Pausing for an instant, Denise invited her mother to come into her bedroom.

Bettie Poole came into her daughter's bedroom pulling a robe over her nightgown. "What's wrong, Honey?" her mother asked.

Denise began to fight back the tears as she started to tell her mother what had happened at the party and how hard she had slapped Darren. She began to feel better as her mother listened without saying much. She gave a nod of assurance after some of the details Denise was telling.

After Denise had told her mother about the events that had happened earlier, her mother assured her, "Honey, don't blame yourself for something you weren't responsible for."

"But Mother, maybe I should have seen it coming. Maybe I shouldn't blame Darren for all of it," Denise answered. "I should have been more aware of his intentions," she continued.

Her mother shook her head and said, "I disagree with you on this matter. You don't try things like Darren tried tonight unless you are sure that both of you want to get involved sexually."

Sitting on the bed together, the two discussed the problem for quite a while. They both started to feel better about where the young couple stood in their relationship to each other.

Denise finally told her mother, "I don't want to date Darren for a while. Until we both understand our commitments with each other, we just won't date."

"I think that is a wise decision, dear. I'm proud of you," her mother added. After pausing for a moment, she got up from the bed and stated, "I hate to see you get hurt like this, but I believe you have made some very big decisions tonight."

As her mother left the room, Denise said, "Thanks, Mom. I'm glad you were here tonight and understand how I feel."

Bettie Poole looked back as she went out the door, and said, "I love you, Denise."

"I love you too, Mom."

Denise showered and dressed for bed. As she turned out the light, she told herself that she had to think about something besides Darren. Taking Mandi's advice, her thoughts turned to the exciting football game they had won.

She pulled up the warm soft covers to go to sleep. As she thought about the game, she remembered Todd's eyes. There appeared to be a loneliness about them tonight.

She had known Todd since he moved to Wills a couple of years earlier. She also knew that his parents had been killed in an airplane crash and that he had moved to this small town to live with his grandfather. Other than that, she knew very little about him.

As she thought of him, she realized how little she knew about this guy. They had only been in a few classes together, and he was always quiet. He didn't answer questions unless he was called upon.

He had attended a few Christian Athletes meetings at the coaches' homes, but always stayed in the background. He never drew attention to himself, but he was the one that had quarterbacked the football team to its first district championship in seventeen years.

There must be more to Todd Perry than his classmates and friends were aware of. Thinking about this quiet quarterback, instead of Darren, Denise slowly dozed off to sleep.

CHAPTER 2

Saturday morning came early as Todd rolled over and looked at the clock. Maybe he shouldn't have read so late last night. When he started reading those western books, he just didn't know when to stop.

Poppy was already up and doing his usual morning jobs. He was out for his morning walk at the moment. He always took a walk in the morning since his last heart attack a year earlier. Unless the weather was bad, he walked every day.

Todd got up and had his breakfast of cereal and milk. He very seldom had bacon and eggs because Poppy had to stay away from that kind of breakfast. After dressing, he headed the few blocks to the field house. He was there with about ten minutes to spare. As he walked in, he noticed everyone was moving rather slowly, just like every Saturday morning. Tough ball games always meant more bruises and sore spots the next day.

Several teammates came from the training room where Coach Willie had performed his usual Saturday morning miracles. There wouldn't be any excuses for not working out this morning. Some were finishing off donuts and Coke as they entered for the morning workout.

Some of the players were playing jokes to get a few laughs. Not everyone enjoyed the jokes because they were still half-asleep. The thing that was of interest this Saturday was seeing the video tape of the championship game.

Tension grew in the room as the tape approached the final part of the game. Even if they did know the outcome of the game, they were still excited when the winning play was run. Everyone hollered and clapped as Todd threw the touchdown pass.

Clay pushed Todd on the shoulder with a lot of force, saying, "Looked like a bullet didn't it, bud?"

Coach Berry also commented, "That's the way championships are won. People have to step forward to make plays like that. The nice thing about it is that everybody had a part in winning the game. Good job, everybody!"

The team then suited out in sweats and helmets and went outside to loosen up. After about thirty minutes of running plays and jogging a few fifties, Coach Berry got everyone together and told them that even though they were two weeks from the playoffs, they must concentrate on this week's game.

Coach Berry paced in front of the team before he spoke. "This Friday is parents' night, and we don't want to let down this week," he cautioned.

With workout over and players heading for the dressing room, Coach Berry mentioned to Todd, "Come by the office on your way home." Todd nodded okay to his coach. Todd got to the office with his hair still wet and his shirt half buttoned.

"Come on in, Todd," Coach said to his quarterback.

"Anything wrong, Coach?" Todd asked.

Coach Berry closed the door and motioned Todd to sit down. "Todd, we had some coaches from Texas Eastern at the game last night. They were impressed by the way you played. They want to see tapes from some of our games, and would like to talk to you when the season is over. If you think you might be interested in playing football for them, let me know and I will contact them for you. You don't have to make a decision now, but just think about it."

"Thanks, Coach, I'll keep it in mind," Todd said. "By the way, Coach," Todd mentioned, "about last night. I really didn't want to run that option left. I was afraid that I might fumble the ball if I had to pitch it. I was sure glad that Stanley was open. I don't mind running it at another time, or at another spot on the field, but when the ball game is on the line, I had rather run something safer."

Coach nodded that he understood, and added, "After looking at last night's tape, we probably would have scored on option left, but we will never know for sure. We won on what we ran, so let's not worry about what is past. You did a good job and I'm proud of you."

As he was leaving, Todd said, "Thanks, Coach. See you Monday."

• • • • • • • • • • • ● • • • • • • • • • • •

The bell rang for Todd's lunch period. He got his tray and went to the table with Clay, Stanley, and Bill.

"Have a seat, bud," Clay said as he pulled out a chair from the table.

"Believe I will," Todd returned as he slowly eased into the seat.

Bill joked, "May I have an autograph?"

Todd blushed as he tried to ignore Bill's joke.

Clay asked Todd if he would like to double date after this Friday's game. The young quarterback said that he didn't think so. "Come on, Todd. Think about it. We've never done anything like that before. We need to do something together."

In order to change the subject, Todd told Clay that he would think about it.

Denise and Mandi also had lunch at this time. As they sat down, Denise could see in the back corner of the lunchroom several of the football players eating. *"Todd and Clay appear to be pretty good friends,"* she thought as she started her lunch.

Mandi asked, "Are you okay after Friday night?"

Denise assured her that she was okay as she continued to glance at Todd's table.

Mandi continued, "Darren told my date, Eddie, that you two had a run-in Friday night."

Denise said, "We are not going to date for a while, so I had rather forget about last Friday."

Mandi said, "That's fine; but what about this Friday? Do you have a date after the game?"

Denise said that she didn't expect to have a date for this week's game.

She hoped that what happened last week would not get around. At least Darren had gone back to college and probably would not be back for a while. He had called her a couple of times, but Denise had not talked to him, so maybe he had taken the hint. She was still bothered by the thought of what had happened.

Denise looked at Todd across the room and wondered about what his life was like. Why did he appear so lonely after the game last week?

She began to wonder why she had never seen him date. He was good looking, at least in her opinion. She could never remember him dating since he had moved here. Could it be because he didn't have a car, or was it because of money? She knew that he lived with his grandfather, and she didn't think they had much money. She also knew that he was a lifeguard at the public swimming pool the last two summers. Several girls had flirted with him, but they never seemed to get anywhere.

She watched Todd and Clay as they left the lunchroom, but Mandi was still talking, so she quickly forgot about the two football players.

· · · · · · · ● · · · · · · · · ·

When Todd finished lunch, he said, "See you guys at practice."

He was leaving the lunch area when Clay said, "Hey, Todd, wait up!" As Clay approached Todd, he said in a low tone, "What's the problem about double dating after the game Friday night? Is it money or something like that?"

As people passed the two athletes, Todd looked around and said, "No, it's not money, Clay. I saved some from lifeguarding this last summer."

Clay was the straight forward type so he continued, "Well, what is the problem then, because something's not right."

Todd didn't say anything as they put up their trays and started down the hall. Finally, when he got to his classroom, he turned to Clay and said, "I'll let you know something at practice this afternoon."

· · · · · · · ● · · · · · · · · ·

With practice over, the sweaty players with dirt caked on their uniforms started off the practice field towards the field house when Clay came up to Todd and stopped him.

"Let me ask you a personal question, and you don't have to answer it if you don't want to, but…have you ever had a date before?"

Todd started toward the field house again. Clay looked at him and said, "That's it, isn't it? You haven't had a date before have you? That's why you're not sure about Friday night; right?"

The six-foot-two, two hundred twenty pound Clay Comer caught Todd at the door, pulled him aside, and said, "I don't want to be nosy, Todd, but you have to start sometime. Man! You are a senior in high school; you can't wait any longer."

Todd stopped and said, "Clay, I haven't had a car or much else to offer a date, and I just never started. I know that it's not going to get any easier."

Clay came back, "I have a date with Cindy for Friday night, and her friend Kim is free. What do you think about letting Cindy set you up? Kim is a good place to start. She won't bite you."

Todd turned pale when he thought about going on a date. Catching his breath, he told Clay, "Okay, let's try it."

Clay paused, "Todd, let's have a good time. Let me know if I can help you. Don't worry about money; we'll rent a movie and go to Cindy's house. Her parents always go to the back of the house and let us have the den to ourselves. We'll pop some popcorn and watch a movie. How does that sound?"

"Sounds good, Clay…sounds good," Todd repeated.

As Clay was leaving the field house, Todd caught him by the shoulder, and said, "Thanks, Clay…I'm looking forward to Friday night."

Clay responded, "See you tomorrow, bud."

On the way home, Todd thought about Kim Carter. She was cute enough, and he knew her as well as anybody. He was thinking about the date for Friday night when his thoughts turned to Denise Poole. "*Man!*" he thought to himself. "*If she wasn't dating that college guy, maybe I could get up the nerve to ask her out sometime. No, I would have to have a car before I could do something like that."* He could see her brown eyes from last Friday, and they still stuck in his mind.

"*Well at least a guy could dream,*" he thought. "*Let's see how this Friday's date goes before I venture out any more. Should I kiss Kim this Friday?*" he wondered. He hadn't thought about that. Would she expect him to? How would he know?

Todd thought to himself, "*You do have common sense, and you will just have to follow your feelings Friday night.*" By the time he got home, his heart was beating rapidly just thinking about having a date Friday night.

• • • • • • • • • ● • • • • • • • • • •

After school, the cheerleaders were working in the cheerleader room putting the finishing touches on the week's breakthrough. "We need to hurry up," Mandi stated. "We have practice in the gym in forty-five minutes."

Denise had put up her brushes and gone to help Mandi put away her equipment. Mandi thanked her for helping. They finished while the rest of the cheerleaders were still busy, so they started to the gym.

"You have a date Friday night?" Denise asked Mandi.

"Yeah," Mandi replied. "What about you?"

Denise said that she didn't have one for the game this week. She then continued, "Mandi, what do you know about Todd Perry?"

Mandi looked up and said, "Why do you ask?"

Denise shrugged her shoulders as she uttered, "I don't know. There was something about him after the championship game that bothered me, but I couldn't tell you what it was."

Mandi said, "Well, for one thing, he's kinda cute."

Denise blushed and said, "Besides that."

Mandi smiled and said, "So! You do think he's cute, don't you?"

Denise couldn't keep from smiling but continued, "What else do you know?"

Mandi said, "Well, he makes good grades, doesn't get in trouble, and usually stays to himself."

The two girls looked at each other for a while, both wondering what the other was thinking. Mandi asked Denise, "What do you know about him?"

Denise replied, "Just what you have told me. Nothing more than that."

They started down the hall to the gym when Mandi asked Denise, "Would you like for me to find out more about him?"

Denise quickly glanced at her friend and stammered, "No! Uh… that's all right, I was just curious, that's all."

The two cheerleaders dropped the subject once they entered the gym for practice. However, Mandi looked at Denise and wondered why her friend was asking about the school's quarterback.

• • • • • • • • • ● • • • • • • • • • •

At Wednesday's practice, Coach Rhodes noticed several players laughing during the drills. Finally he called one of the players over and asked, "What is so funny? Y'all have been laughing about something ever since we hit the field."

Bill hesitated, but finally came out with it, "Okay Coach, you'll find out, anyway. Pat found a dead mouse in the dressing room and put it in Stanley's shoe. He put the shoe on and never noticed that something was in it. Every now and then, he shakes his foot like there is something wrong. We didn't expect it to go this long."

Coach Rhodes shook his head and said, "You guys! What will you come up with next? You people are always playing a joke on somebody. One of these days, someone is going to get even."

Bill watched as Coach Rhodes went to Coach Berry and told him about the mouse. He was relieved when they both giggled and looked at Stanley.

In the dressing room after practice, the coaches heard an explosion of laughter and ran to see what was happening. Stanley and another player were heading to the rest room. Both players were in a hurry and both were gagging. Coach Berry asked what had happened. Everyone was laughing so hard that they couldn't talk.

Bill, rubbing the tears from his eyes, was finally able to talk. "Coach, Stanley took his shoe off and found the dead mouse. He and Pat are throwing up in the restroom."

Everyone in the field house could hear the two throwing up on the other side of the restroom wall. The coach grinned and went to Stanley's locker and looked at the shoe. Just visible was a small, mutilated mouse that had been ground into the player's shoe. The stench was so strong that Coach Berry almost gagged himself.

The coach walked over to the trash barrel and dropped the shoe into the trash. Then he turned and hollered to Coach Willie, "Coach, get Stanley another pair of shoes! I think his feet stink too bad to wear this pair again."

Bill was still laughing, but commented, "Did you see the expression on Stanley's face when he saw that mouse!"

Another player, also laughing, said, "Yeah, and did you see him when that smell hit him?"

Stanley was not laughing as he came from the restroom. His sneer was enough to send chills up Bill's back.

Everyone with the exception of Stanley and Pat were still giggling as Clay and Todd left the field house. Clay remarked, "I didn't know they ate so much for lunch."

Todd laughed as he joked, "There must have been some breakfast still in them."

Clay then said, "Would you like a ride home?"

"You bet," Todd replied.

The trip to Todd's house was short, and as Todd was getting out of the car, Clay said, "I'll pick you up Friday at five to go to the field house. Tell Poppy that you'll be late Friday night."

Todd said, "I've already told him that I have a date. I think he was glad about it. He has been concerned that I haven't dated before." After pausing for a moment, Todd said, "Thanks, Clay."

"Sure thing, bud. See you at school tomorrow."

· · · · · · • · · · · · · ·

Todd finished his homework in math and picked up his western book to read some more about survival in the west. Poppy was going to bed and told Todd that he would see him in the morning.

He opened his book, but his thoughts turned to his date Friday night. Kim was an attractive junior, and Todd only knew her through school activities. She was active in student council and was a member of the high school drill team. He just hoped that he didn't embarrass himself on the date.

Todd knew that he would have to watch Clay closely and try to take any hints from him that he might pick up. In a way, Todd began to get a little excited. He knew sooner or later he would be dating. He wondered how many seniors in high school had never had a date. He knew that there couldn't be very many. Friday night after the football game, he knew that there would be one less on that list.

Sitting in his recliner with his book now face down on his lap, Todd was thinking about not having a car. He could have had all kinds of dates and girlfriends if only—He then said to himself, *"Todd, you can fret about this all you want to, but it's not going to change a thing."*

Todd's parents had set up a trust fund in their will for him when he turned eighteen. He would reach his eighteenth birthday in March. At that time, he knew he would be getting a large sum of money from that will. He didn't know exactly how much, but he knew that with his parents' insurance money, his college education would be secure.

When he received this money, he would be able to get himself a car, new clothes, and anything else that he needed, or wanted. That wasn't going to help him at this point, but he knew that he would be more secure financially after he turned eighteen. As far as he knew, Poppy was the only person in town that knew about the fund. He was thankful his parents had taken care of his future before they had been killed.

·········●·········

The time spent waiting for a game was always hard on Todd. His stomach turned over; he couldn't sit still. Everyone was always so serious. In fact, some of the players, like Clay, wouldn't talk to anybody.

Coach Berry finally called the quarterbacks into his office to go over final details about the game plan. "Remember," Coach Berry said, "if there is any confusion when the play is brought in, just pat your hand on the top of your helmet and call your own play. If we are at a critical time in the game, we will call a time out. By the way, Todd, don't pat your helmet on option left."

When Todd looked up at the coach, he saw him smiling. Todd knew that the coach remembered what he had told him about the option play last week. He smiled back at the coach.

Coach Berry had been such a big influence on Todd. He felt like he could go to him with just about any problem. In fact, he may have been as close to a father as Todd had known since his parent's tragedy.

After the pre-game warm-up, the senior players and cheerleaders lined up with their parents under the goalposts. Poppy proudly took his place beside his grandson.

Being in alphabetical order, Todd was closer to the end of the line than he was to the front. As he glanced over his shoulder, he looked right into the brown eyes of Denise Poole. He tried to talk, but he found himself more or less stuttering when all he could say was, "Uh...hello."

Turning back to face the front of the line, he thought to himself, *"Boy, did you leave a good impression or what?"*

Wondering how to get his composure back, he tried to think of some way to make conversation, when Denise said, "Todd, I would like for you to meet my parents, Don and Bettie Poole. Mom, Dad, this is Todd Perry."

Todd and Mr. Poole shook hands, and Todd was able to get out, "Nice to meet you, sir." Todd then introduced the Poole family to Poppy, who was beside him.

Mr. Poole mentioned to Todd how much he enjoyed last week's game and how the touchdown pass made it so exciting.

Todd blushed as he gave Mr. Poole his, "Thank you, sir."

By this time, the announcer was introducing the players and cheerleaders along with their parents, or in Todd's situation, a representative. Todd knew that his parents would have been proud of him and would have cherished this moment.

Todd felt proud when the announcer introduced him as, "The son of the late Sherry and Philip Todd Perry. He is being escorted tonight by his grandfather, William 'Poppy' Perry." They walked to the middle of the field, followed by the Poole family.

With the pre-game ceremonies behind them, the players huddled to get ready for the game. The Wills Wildcats were already district champs and in the playoffs; this was the last regular season game for both teams.

The Wildcats received the kickoff and had the football first. Todd and the rest of the offense had moved the ball down the field and had first down on the opponent's twenty three yard line when Stanley came from the sideline with the play, "Pro right, option left." Todd glanced at the sideline and Coach Berry, who had a big grin on his face.

Todd took the snap and started down the line of scrimmage. When the defensive end tried to cover the pitch man on the option, Todd cut upfield. The hole opened up just as he exploded toward the end zone. Stanley had the last tackler tied up, so Todd cut outside of his block and sprinted into the end zone for the touchdown.

The Wildcats had scored first. After the extra point, Todd moved to the sideline where Coach Berry was all smiles. "Nice play, Todd. Good job," his coach commented.

Todd knew that Coach was glad that the touchdown had come off of the option play.

Todd didn't play much more than half of the game because next week they would be in the playoffs. When he was finished for the night, Todd had scored on the option play and thrown a touchdown pass to Stanley. The Wildcats went on to win the game twenty-one to seven.

After the game, the players huddled in the middle of the field for prayer. Cindy met Clay, and Kim met Todd as they all dropped to one knee for the coach's prayer.

When they got up, Todd noticed that a lot of people had come on the field following the game. As he and Kim started off the field, he thought of how winning would get people involved. They really enjoyed the feeling of victory.

Kim put her arm around Todd, and so he did likewise.

Todd thought to himself, "*Hey, this is all right. Maybe I should have had a date after a game before. This feels pretty good.*"

Before they reached the end of the field, he noticed that Denise didn't have her college guy with her tonight. As they passed, Denise looked at Todd and told him that he had played a good game.

Denise had noticed Kim walking Todd off the field after the team prayer and wondered when this had started. She thought to herself, "*I believe that this is the first time I've ever seen him with a girl. Maybe he does date, and I just haven't noticed it.*"

As Todd and Kim passed through the gate, he heard the usual, "Nice game, son," and he knew the source of those words. He looked over at Poppy and gave him a thumbs up to let him know that he had heard him. Todd told Kim to wait in front, and he would be out shortly with Clay.

·········●·········

At Cindy's house, Todd found himself buried deeply into the corner of the big plush couch with Kim about as close as she could get to him, and he had put his arm around her because it seemed like the thing to do.

He was watching Cindy and Clay very closely on the other end of the couch. "*It is amazing how four people can fit on this couch and still leave so much room in the middle of it,*" Todd thought to himself.

Todd found it hard to eat popcorn and drink a coke with only his left hand, but he was enjoying Kim's closeness. When his arm began to go to sleep, he knew that sooner or later he was going to have to move it, but when and how he was going to do it without disturbing Kim was quickly becoming a problem.

He had noticed that Clay and Cindy weren't the least bit interested in the movie. "*Wow! Clay, you have to breathe sometimes,*"

Todd thought. *"Does Kim expect to be kissed?"* Todd wondered. He was almost afraid to move, but that arm had to be losing circulation, he thought.

About the time he thought he was suffering the most, Kim looked at him just right, and before he knew it, their lips were touching. They were kissing! Todd's limp arm reached around Kim and he lost all thought of reality.

"Wow!" Todd thought. *"Wow...man!"*

As the movie ended, Todd realized that he knew nothing about how it had turned out. This had eased his anxiety about dating. Maybe he and Clay could try this again, and soon. Maybe this time he would approach Clay about dating girls together.

Todd walked Kim to the door as Clay and Cindy waited in the car. He put his arms around Kim and felt her warm body next to his. He kissed her several times before she went inside. He was feeling good about himself as he approached the car, thinking, *"Maybe I'm a fast learner!"*

Clay and Cindy dropped Todd off at Poppy's house a few minutes later. Todd told Clay how much he had enjoyed the evening.

Clay didn't say a whole lot, but he knew that Todd had really enjoyed himself on the date. "See you at practice," Clay said.

Todd replied, "Sure thing, see you at practice."

The night was getting rather chilly by now, but Todd lingered outside for a while thinking about his date. He didn't think he and Kim would ever be serious about each other, but he did enjoy being with her tonight.

He had to admit that he liked kissing her. He wondered if different girls kissed differently? What about Denise? How would she kiss? Denise really looked nice tonight at the pre-game ceremony. Todd began to think about putting his arms around her waist and looking into those brown eyes, and...wow! *"I need to get in bed, it's getting late!"* he realized.

CHAPTER 3

When Todd's clock went off about nine-thirty, he lay in bed thinking about the previous night. He slowly got out of bed and started searching for something to wear. The weather was cold and drizzly outside, so Todd found something warm to put on. He didn't fix breakfast because he was running a little late. He realized he should have gotten up early enough to call Clay; maybe he would have picked him up this morning.

Too late now. He grabbed a snack and started out the door. Poppy, coming in from his morning walk, greeted him with, "Make sure you have enough on because it's getting colder outside."

Todd responded, "Thanks, but I'm okay."

Todd came in as several others were arriving at the field house. Clay was already suited out and sitting in his locker when Todd came in and started to get ready. Todd watched as Stanley pulled something out of his locker and said, "Hey, someone left a mouse pad...Man! Somebody has a twisted sense of humor around here." Players slowly realized the meaning of the "mouse" pad and started snickering.

Most players were fairly alert this morning since they had only played about half a game the night before. Coach Rhodes stepped in and said, "Okay, guys, let's get outside. We'll just be out there long enough to loosen up this morning. Coach Berry is going to stay in and help with the scouting report."

After about thirty minutes of drills and running a few plays, everyone went back into the dressing room. When they were through showering and getting dressed, they went to the film room to watch last night's game video. Todd and Clay lay down on the floor together.

Clay said to Todd, "Make sure you watch the *end* of this tape." He smiled as Todd began to blush.

After the game video, Coach Berry came in with the scouting report. "Guys, this is a very good football team we play next week. We can't take Rush City lightly. We will have to be prepared for the game. It will be played in Dallas next Friday night. We'll give you the times later. We must work hard all week."

After the morning workout, Todd and Clay were by their lockers when Todd asked, "What did you mean when you told me to be sure to watch the end of this tape?"

Clay looked at his friend and said, "Bud, you had no idea how that movie ended last night. You were too wrapped up with Kim."

Todd blushed slightly as he said, "You're a fine one to be talking. You didn't breathe during the whole film."

They joked with each other for a while, and finally Clay said, "Come on; I'll give you a ride home."

At Todd's house, Clay mentioned, "Todd, if you ever need to borrow my car, just let me know. I can always use my parents'."

Todd paused a moment and said, "Thanks Clay, but I don't have my driver's license."

Clay said, "Gosh, I never thought about…Well, anytime you want to double date, just let me know."

Todd said, "I really enjoyed last night and wish we could do it this week, but we'll get back too late to go out."

Clay remarked, "We'll work out something later. See you Monday."

As Clay drove off, Todd went inside his house thinking about this coming weekend. He now knew that dating was fun, and he will have to plan his next date. Who could he ask out next time? Kim? Denise? Who would it be?

•••••••●•••••••

Monday after practice, Coach Berry stopped Todd on the way home and asked, "Todd, we are having a Christian Athletes meeting at our house tonight and wondered if you would like to come?"

Todd thought a minute and said "Sure, what time?"

"Seven o'clock. I'll have Coach Rhodes pick you up on the way to the meeting."

Todd thanked him and left for home. On the way, he thought about other Christian Athletes meetings. They were usually fun, and he did enjoy being with everyone. He didn't go to church very often, so he didn't have a very good understanding of what the leaders talked about most of the time. However, this would give him a chance to get out of the house and have something to do that evening.

There were about twenty-five athletes at Coach Berry's house when Todd got there. Everyone was glad he had come to the meeting and made him feel welcome. He was getting some cookies and punch when he bumped into Denise Poole.

She turned around and said, "Well, hello, Todd. It's good to see you here tonight."

Todd replied, "Thanks." She invited him to sit down with her and Mandi. Todd didn't hesitate to join the two attractive girls.

The program that night was about Christian dating. Todd blushed a few times, thinking about his date with Kim, but he felt that they both had had a good time at Cindy's house.

After the program, the athletes visited and had a good time being together. He was able to be with Denise some of the time, but people moved around in order to visit with everyone.

Todd enjoyed being with people, but he would have liked to have spent more time with Denise. For some reason, he didn't isolate himself tonight. He was beginning to enjoy being with his classmates. He didn't know what the difference was, but he seemed to be more comfortable with his peers tonight.

When Coach Rhodes dropped him off at his house after the meeting, Todd thought as he walked up to the porch, *"Denise gets better looking every time I see her."* She also seemed to be a sincere person. He thought maybe he should get to know her better, but he didn't know how he could date her with his limited sources. Well, perhaps some day he could find a way.

· · · · · · • · · · · · ·

On Thursday night, the school and community set up a bonfire and pep rally. Everyone was excited about the big event. After practice on Thursday, Clay asked if Todd needed a ride to the pep rally.

Todd answered, "Sure, what time do I need to be ready?"

Clay said, "Well...it starts at seven-thirty; how about picking you up about seven-fifteen?"

Todd replied, "Sounds good to me. See you then."

As Todd was leaving, Clay said, "Hey, by the way, Cindy and Kim may be there!"

Todd hesitated, then said, "Okay." He wondered if it was a very good idea to be with Kim at the pep rally. The cheerleaders were leading it, and he knew that Denise would see him. However, he didn't know Denise that well and probably wouldn't for a while, if ever. He wondered if she would be out of his league with all of the money her family seemed to have.

· · · · · · · ● · · · · · · · ·

Denise was at the gym getting ready for the pep rally when Mandi came in.

Mandi asked, "Need some help?"

"Sure, grab those megaphones."

Mandi continued, "This is a good night for a bonfire...nice and cold! Too bad we don't have anyone to cuddle up to."

Denise replied, "Well, maybe the fire will keep us warm."

Mandi came back, "Yeah, but that's not near as much fun."

· · · · · · · ● · · · · · · · ·

The band was playing as Todd and Clay arrived at the big pep rally. It was fairly cold that night, but both of the football players had on their letterman's jackets. Maybe they should have worn more clothes or heavier jackets, but that wouldn't have looked as macho, Todd thought.

The cheerleaders started the pep rally a few minutes behind time because a large number of fans from town were coming in late.

Clay and Todd stood watching as the cheerleaders were leading their first cheer. Naturally, Todd was admiring Denise when he mumbled aloud to himself, "Man, isn't she easy to look at!"

Clay turned around and asked Todd, "What did you say?"

Todd, startled that Clay might have heard him, quickly replied, "Oh…uh…nothing!"

Clay came back, "Yes you did; what did you say?"

Todd exclaimed, "I didn't say anything!"

"Well it sure did sound like you said something."

Todd knew he was blushing, but he continued to watch Denise as the cheerleaders led the crowd during the pep rally.

After a couple of yells, Cindy and Kim arrived at the pep rally. Cindy moved up next to Clay, while Kim moved next to Todd. They all smiled at each other as the ceremony continued.

When the band had finished playing the school fight song, Mandi stepped forward and yelled, "We want to hear from seniors Todd Perry and Clay Comer!"

Everyone yelled their approval as Clay led Todd to the front of the crowd. Todd was wishing they had given him some warning in order for him to have prepared a speech.

Denise was standing in line with the rest of the cheerleading group thinking how nice Todd looked in his letterman's jacket. His six-foot-three-inch frame stood out as he moved in front of the pep rally. She cautiously looked around to see if anyone had noticed her admiring the handsome football player.

Clay pushed Todd forward as the crowd got quiet. Todd hesitated, shuffled his feet, and finally said, "I'd like to thank everyone for coming out tonight. Be sure to come to the game tomorrow night and help us win bi-district!" The crowd hollered their approval of the quarterback's words as Todd stepped aside and let Clay take over.

Clay was more aggressive as he stepped forward; he yelled, "We want to bash some heads!" That brought a loud roar from the fans. The two players took their place by Kim and Cindy after their speeches. The coaches then stepped forward to light the fire.

Denise, standing in front of the fire, didn't notice Kim beside Todd until the bonfire got rather bright. She thought, "*I wonder if they are going together.*" She tried to put the thought out of her mind as the fans started to move around the fire. She couldn't help watching Todd and Kim during the rest of the evening.

Clay asked Todd if he wanted to take the girls home after the pep rally, and Todd accepted the offer. They piled into Clay's car after the bonfire was going down and went to the local hangout.

A large number of students were there after the pep rally. Mandi and Denise arrived just as Todd, Kim, Clay, and Cindy were getting their drinks. Todd and Denise looked right at each other when the two girls entered the room. Todd knew he looked self-conscious and tried to muster up a smile, and Denise was just as uneasy.

Denise wondered why she felt this way over someone she had never dated. Did she want to know Todd better, or was it the fact that he was with another girl that made her feel that way? Whatever the problem, she sure didn't like this feeling.

Todd was restless and didn't think that they would ever leave the joint. He couldn't understand why he was so uncomfortable. He wasn't even sure Denise would want to date him. Anyway, he was glad when Clay finally got ready to leave.

The two couples climbed into Clay's 1965 Mustang and rode around for a few minutes, but with the biggest game of their lives coming up, they knew that they had to get to bed early tonight. They took the girls home without being out very long.

Kim was the first to go home. Todd enjoyed taking her to the door and kissing her good night. He spent more time at the door than he intended, so he was a little embarrassed when he finally got to the car. However, when he got there, he knew that Clay and Cindy hadn't waited for him. They were all wrapped up in each other's arms.

Todd couldn't pass up the chance to sneak up and startle the couple when he banged his hand on the side of Clay's car door. Both jumped and laughed as Todd got in the car. "Miss me?" Todd asked.

Cindy was a little embarrassed, but Clay commented, "I thought you were going to stay all night."

Clay and Cindy took Todd home next and told him to get a good night's sleep. Todd assumed that he would try, but going to sleep on a night like this wasn't going to be easy. He was keyed up from the pep rally, he had kissed Kim goodnight, and then to top it all off, he kept thinking about Denise. "What a night!"

Todd finally got in bed after having a small snack. He rolled and tossed for what seemed like an eternity. His mind wandered through the evening, the pep rally, Kim, Denise, and then the ball game. He lay there and tried to relax, but the more he tried to go to sleep, the more he would get excited. He slowly began to doze and finally drifted off into a restless sleep.

• • • • • • • • • ● • • • • • • • • •

School on Friday was hard for Todd. He couldn't keep his mind on the lessons. He didn't get much sleep the previous night; his mind kept going back and forth between Kim and Denise. Above everything else, he was nervous about the big game that they were going to play tonight.

At long last, the time came for all of the players to load the bus for the game. Todd and Stanley sat together on the way. They talked about pass patterns and blocking assignments. Todd noticed that Stanley had gotten quiet. Turning to his receiver, Todd found that Stanley had dozed off to sleep. Being a little sleepy himself, Todd dozed off into a relaxing sleep, too.

As the bus drove up into the parking lot, Todd woke up. "*Man!*" he told himself, "*I feel worse now than I did before I went to sleep.*" He tried to stretch and loosen up, but it was going to take a few minutes to get his senses back.

The players slowly got off the bus and began to gather the travel bags that held their equipment. After putting their bags into lockers, several of them walked to the field. The coaches were already setting up training equipment and sideline phones. Coaches seemed to enjoy setting up for football games. Todd could never understand if they really liked to do this or if it was just a way to cover up their own nervousness.

Todd looked around and noticed that the opponents were also on the field. "*Man, they look awfully big!*" Todd thought.

As if reading his mind, Coach Berry told Todd, "We look big to them, also."

Todd smiled at him, and said, "Thanks Coach, I needed to hear that."

Players soon returned to the dressing room to get ready for the game. Todd felt more tension tonight than in the previous games. He noticed that his heartbeat was faster, and he couldn't seem to settle down. He was glad to start putting on his uniform. He felt even better when it finally came time to go out for warm-ups. For the first time since they arrived, he began to get mentally ready to play.

Clay, Todd, and Stanley were the team captains for tonight's game. As they approached the middle of the field for the coin toss, fans on both sidelines yelled for their respective teams. Todd noticed that the other team looked just as nervous as he felt. The Wildcats lost the coin toss and would have to kick off, which meant that Todd would have to wait a while longer before getting on the field to play.

Excitement was unbelievable as the teams ran through their breakthroughs for the start of the game. Both teams lined up for the national anthem, and Todd felt like the game would never get started. Finally, the game began with the Wildcats kicking off the football.

Both teams were having trouble moving the football when the Rush City Ponies completed a long pass for a touchdown. It had happened so fast that the Wildcats were caught by surprise. Now they were behind. The score stayed 7 to 0 until late in the fourth quarter.

The Wildcats had the ball on their own thirty-eight yard line, with third down and eight yards to go for a first down. Coach Berry called for a sideline pass to Stanley. As Todd dropped back to pass, the defensive end behind him made contact just as he was throwing the ball. The poorly thrown pass was picked off by the defensive cornerback, who went untouched into the end zone. Todd was helpless to do anything but lie there and watch the Ponies score the touchdown.

"No!" Todd hollered, "No!" He couldn't believe what was happening. He didn't want to leave the field. There had to be a flag or something to change the play. Todd looked around, but there was no flag. They had scored on his interception.

When he got to the sideline, Coach Berry told him, "Good effort, Todd. They just made a great play."

That didn't help much. Todd felt as though he was going to throw up. It had never entered his mind that they might be beaten tonight. There were seven minutes left in the game, and they were down 14 to 0.

On the next possession, the Wildcats moved the ball sixty-five yards and scored on a twelve yard touchdown pass from Todd to Stanley. There were only forty-one seconds left in the game. Everything was riding on an ensuing kickoff. Fans on both sidelines were standing and yelling.

Denise was on the sideline near Todd and could see the hurt in his face. It would be so easy to walk over to him and try to console his hurt, but she knew that was out of the question. She stood in the background and watched him as he moved back over next to his coach.

All players, coaches and cheerleaders were jamming the sidelines as the ball was being kicked. Following the on-side kick, the scramble for the ball was furious. Both sides knew that the outcome of the game might be determined by the last position of the football. As the officials unpiled the stack of players, everyone from Wills was disappointed to see that the ball belonged to the Rush City Ponies.

"*That's it! The game's over,*" Todd thought. He was stunned as the clock ran out. They had lost the bi-district game.

"*It just couldn't happen,*" Todd thought. He looked at Clay, who was sitting on the ground with a blank stare on his face.

Coach Berry said, "Okay everybody, shake their hands... everyone to the middle of the field." Todd really didn't want to go, but he knew that he had to meet the victors. After shaking hands, all of the players from both sides knelt for a prayer.

After the prayer, Todd was so stunned that he wandered off by himself to the goal post at the far end of the field. He stood there with his helmet in his passing hand, thinking of how the game could have ended if he hadn't thrown that interception. He couldn't believe that the game had ended this way. It just wasn't possible.

Players were scattered over the field. He turned to walk to the dressing room when he noticed that Denise was right behind him. They stared at each other for a moment. She put her hand on his arm and softly said, "You played a good game tonight, Todd. I'm proud of you."

Todd was embarrassed that he had tears in his eyes, but he said to her, "Thanks, Denise." Deep down, he wished that he could grab her and hold her in his arms for a while.

They walked to the dressing room side by side. Neither said very much, but it was nice just to be close as they left the field.

It took the team longer to shower and get dressed tonight. The seniors couldn't believe that they had played their last high school football game. It wasn't supposed to end like this. The realization was slowly sinking in to the seniors as they loaded their bags on the bus.

・・・・・・・●・・・・・・・

The steaks were hard to swallow as they sat quietly eating their after-game meal. Clay and Stanley were eating with Todd, and nobody wanted to talk. The coaches went around and tried to tell everyone that they had finished a good season, but that didn't seem to help the dejected players very much.

The cheerleaders were also eating with the team. As they were all leaving together, Todd made a point to find Denise. He looked into her dark brown eyes and said, "Thanks for coming by after the game. Sorry that I wasn't very friendly, but I do appreciate your concern."

Denise dropped her head and replied, "I understand, Todd. It was a difficult time. We all felt bad, but you *were* very good tonight. Try not to feel too bad about the game."

Todd thanked her and went to the bus.

He again felt sick on the way home. His thoughts kept going back to the pass that had been intercepted and returned for a touchdown. What could he have done differently? Every time he visualized that play, he would feel a knot in his stomach.

Todd knew that he had to think of something more pleasant. What could be more pleasant than thinking about Denise Poole? He was glad that he had taken the opportunity to talk to her. It wasn't as hard as he had thought it would be. Maybe he would be able to find something to talk to her about in the future. He still couldn't forget how attractive she had become to him.

• • • • • • • • ● • • • • • • • • •

It didn't seem right Monday not to have football practice. The basketball coach had talked to Todd about playing basketball. The coach had told him to take a few days off and get some rest before starting the new sport. Todd went to the field house to talk to Coach Berry. He felt a need to discuss his future.

It was quiet when he walked into the empty dressing room. Equipment was stacked on the floor while coaches and managers were taking inventory and storing it for next season. When Coach Berry saw Todd, he said, "Hey, come in."

Todd asked his coach if he could talk to him in private. Coach Berry invited him to his office and closed the door. After they both sat down, Todd started the conversation. "Coach, has anyone shown any more interest in my playing college football?"

Coach Berry told Todd that he had sent tapes to three schools that had shown interest in him.

"Coach," Todd continued, "there is something I've never told anyone before. My parents…uh…left me a trust fund that will be mine when I turn eighteen. I don't know exactly how much it is, but it will be quite a large amount. They tried to take care of my future while I was young."

Coach Berry told Todd, "I'm glad to hear that. I was really worried about what you were going to do next year if one of those schools didn't come through with a scholarship. I feel good about your ability to play college-level football."

Todd continued, "Coach, when I reach eighteen, I may need some help taking care of things. Could I call on you if I need some help?"

Coach Berry smiled and said, "I would be glad to do anything I can to help you."

Todd replied, "Thanks, Coach. I may be calling on you."

Clay came in the field house as Coach Berry and Todd were finishing their conversation. The three talked about the game last week and how much they had enjoyed the season. They rehashed the game and things that might have made a difference in the outcome.

The coach asked Clay about his plans for the next school year. Clay was unsure about what he was going to do. He wanted to play football again but didn't know where he might be able to go. Coach Berry asked Clay, "Would you like for me to check with schools that are recruiting Todd to see if some of them might also take a look at you?"

Clay perked up and replied, "Sure! I would love to have the chance to play again. It would be great if I could play with Todd."

The coach assured him that there would be no guarantees, but he would see what he could do. Clay thanked him as they got up to leave.

When they started out the door, Coach Berry told both boys that he had enjoyed coaching them and that he would always be around if he could help them. Both players shook hands with their coach and thanked him. Todd and Clay were wishing that this football season still had another game to play.

On the way out, Clay offered Todd a ride home, and Todd was glad to accept.

They decided to go get a drink at the local hangout. On the way, Clay mentioned to Todd about the school dance that the Student Council was sponsoring next Friday night. He asked Todd if he wanted to double date again.

Todd thought for a few moments. He reasoned, "If I go with Kim, Denise may come by herself. If that happened, then I would not be free to be with her. If I don't have a date, I'll be free to visit with both girls." Finally, Todd told Clay, "I don't think I'll have a date for the dance this week."

Clay was puzzled about why Todd didn't want to have a date. Clay, being the type he was, said, "Okay! Out with it Todd! Why don't you want to have a date Friday?"

Todd told Clay, "It's not what you think, Clay. I'm not afraid to date anymore. I would like to be free to visit with other girls this week if possible."

Clay paused for a moment, and came back, "Is there something you're not telling me?"

Todd really wanted to talk to his friend about Denise, but was still unsure of what his own intentions were. He knew that Denise was from a well-to-do family, and he didn't know what kind of position that put him in if he wanted to pursue seeing her.

Todd knew that Denise hadn't seen Darren for a while, and he felt good about that. He had never liked Darren from the beginning. This college student had always been stuck on himself and, in Todd's opinion, was just downright snobby. Todd always thought that Denise could do better than Darren, anyway.

As Clay and Todd entered the hangout, Clay teased Todd, "Bud, you're hiding something from old Clay. You know that I'll find out sooner or later, don't you?"

Todd said, "Probably, but for now let's just forget about it."

Clay exclaimed, "There! I knew it! There is something you're not telling me!"

The two friends gave each other a hard time as they drank their cokes and visited with other friends. Every time Clay got the chance, he would try to trick Todd. "Hey Todd," Clay commented, "who did you say you were going with Friday night?"

Todd grinned and said, "I don't have a date Friday night, Clay."

Clay responded in a disappointed manner, "Oh, that's right. I forgot."

A few minutes later, Clay asked Todd, "Hey, Bud! Who walked you off the field Friday night?"

A little shocked, Todd replied cautiously, "I don't remember anybody walking me off the field."

He was relieved when Clay replied, "Oh, sorry about that."

Todd knew that Clay had hit close to home on that try. He decided that he had better get home before his friend got some information that he didn't want him to have.

Clay drove Todd home, and as he was leaving, he commented, "It's not nice to try to fool Clay Comer. I guess I will have to do some more investigating on this little matter."

Todd smiled as Clay drove off. He had really wanted to confide in Clay about Denise, but it was a lot of fun leading him on like this. He hadn't realized how curious Clay had been. He knew that Clay would spend the rest of the week trying to find out what Todd was up to. This was going to be a fun week after all.

CHAPTER 4

Wednesday at lunch, Clay found Todd in the lunchroom sitting with his usual buddies. They were discussing how different the week could have been if they had won the game last Friday. Clay worked his way into a spot at the table and asked Todd, "Have you changed your mind about the dance Friday night?"

Todd smiled at Clay and said, "Nope!" Todd knew that Clay was getting more curious.

Clay looked at Todd and said, "Something's not right here. You're acting like this is top secret. I think you should let me in on what's happening."

Todd replied, "Why do you think there is a secret?"

Clay responded, "You had too much fun with Kim not to have a date for the dance."

As Clay became more and more curious, Todd said, "Clay, stop worrying. I'm not up to anything. You're just imagining things."

Clay shook his head in disgust.

The two friends had finished lunch and started to their classes when Clay stopped Todd and said, "Seriously, Todd, Kim would really like to go with you Friday night. Do you think you might reconsider?"

Todd explained, "Clay, I would like to be free Friday to visit with other people. I plan on seeing Kim at the dance, but right now I don't want to be tied down to any one person."

Clay left shaking his head again and remarked, "Okay, I hope you have a good time at the dance."

• • • • • • • • ● • • • • • • • • •

Denise and Mandi were working in the cheerleader room while they were eating lunch. Football season was over, and they were getting ready for the upcoming basketball season. Mandi asked Denise, "Are you going to the dance Friday night?"

Denise replied, "I wouldn't miss it."

Mandi continued, "Do you have a date?"

Denise remarked, "Not this week. I've gone with Darren so long that I'm actually looking forward to going by myself. Do you have a date?"

Mandi replied, "Yes, I'm going with Eddie." Mandi paused a moment and continued, "Denise, I noticed you talking to Todd after the game last week. Are you two becoming friends?"

Denise, slightly surprised, said, "We have talked to each other a few times, but that's all there is to it. He was by himself after the game, and I felt he needed a friend."

Mandi agreed, "Yeah, I felt sorry for him after that interception."

Denise said, "I did, too, and since he doesn't have a family, I had an urge to go to him after the game. It was obvious he was hurting pretty badly."

The two girls were through cleaning up when the bell rang for the next period. Mandi was the first out; and as she left the room, she turned around and commented, "You two looked cute together."

Denise quickly looked up with her mouth half open, and stared at Mandi in surprise. Mandi winked at her and smiled as she stepped into the crowded hall.

Denise, in the room by herself, thought about what her friend had implied. She wondered, *Did she see more than I thought she did? Why did she make that comment? Well... Todd is cute.*

Leaving the cheerleader room, Denise wondered if Todd would have a date with Kim, Friday. There wasn't any way to find out without being nosy. She would just have to wait until the dance to find out.

· · · · · · · ● · · · · · · · · ·

The school bell rang, ending the day. Normally, Todd would be at football practice at this time of the day, and next week he would probably be at basketball practice. However, today he stayed and visited with the counselor about where he wanted to go to school next year.

He was in the vicinity of the gym when he saw Denise. He made it a point to be close enough to talk to her. She was on the way to the cheerleader room, which was on the other side of the gym. Todd started the conversation by saying, "Thanks for walking off the field with me after the game Friday night. It meant a lot to be with someone after losing like we did."

They worked their way through the crowd as Denise said, "I felt bad after the game, but I couldn't imagine how you must have felt. I just felt an urge to walk with you when you left the field."

Todd felt out of place talking to Denise at school with everyone around. Deep down he wanted to ask her if she was going to the dance Friday night, but that would sound as if he wanted to ask her for a date. He knew he didn't have the means to do that at this time.

They walked to the cheerleader room, where he left her. As he left, he thought about how he might approach her at the dance Friday night. What if she had a date? Maybe she wouldn't come unless she had a date? He knew he wanted to be there when she arrived; then he could make the decision about how he would ask her to dance.

"Hey Bud!" Clay called, "We need to have a talk." Todd realized that Clay had seen him talking to Denise and was going to question him.

Todd responded, "What's up, Clay?"

Clay said, "You are! Did I just see you walking Denise Poole to the cheerleader room?"

Todd responded, "Yep! You sure did."

Clay hesitated a moment and said, "That's why you don't want to have a date with Kim this week, isn't it?"

Todd asked Clay, "Could we go get a drink or something?"

Clay responded, "Let's go!"

When the two buddies got in the car, Clay commented, "Okay, talk to me. Are you interested in Denise? She is good looking, and her family has plenty of money, you know."

They started down the street in Clay's Mustang as Todd started the conversation. He told Clay he first began to notice Denise after the championship game. He mentioned how she had followed him to the end of the field after they got beat last week and then walked him to the dressing room. Todd continued, "We don't have anything going between us, but we have talked to each other a few times."

Clay interrupted, "Do you want to ask her for a date Friday night?"

Todd said, "I don't think I'm ready for that yet. Let's wait until after the dance and see what happens."

Clay asked, "What happens if someone else asks her?"

Todd replied, "I've thought about that and decided to take my chances."

They stopped at the local hangout and started to get out of the car, when Todd grabbed Clay's arm and said, "Clay, I hope you won't say anything to anybody about this conversation."

Clay said, "Don't worry; I won't breathe a word...Hey, Stanley!... Guess what?"

Todd was about to panic, when Clay told Stanley, "I talked to Coach the other day about possibly playing college football." He looked at the blushing Todd and snickered, "Gotcha!"

• • • • • • • ● • • • • • • • • •

Denise had just finished her homework when the telephone rang. Her mother came to her room and said, "It's Darren! Do you want to talk to him?"

Denise thought a moment and said, "I'll have to face him sooner or later. I guess this is as good a time as any."

She took the phone and said, "Hello."

Darren replied, "Hello Denise, I didn't know if you would speak to me or not...I want to apologize for the way I acted at the party. I was wrong and am truly sorry."

Denise said, "Darren, I'm sorry I hit you like I did. I didn't mean to hurt you. I just wanted you to stop being so...uh...forward."

He replied, "Well...I think I deserved it."

They talked for several minutes, and Darren finally asked, "Would you let me take you to the dance Friday night?"

Denise hesitated a moment and said, "Not this week Darren, maybe later. I still need a little more time to get over this before we start dating again."

Darren responded, "Well, I can't say that I blame you, but I wish you would reconsider. If not this week, maybe next week? I will be coming home for Thanksgiving at that time."

Denise replied, "You can give me a call when you get home, and we'll talk about it."

Darren said, "I'll call you as soon as I get home."

As she hung up the phone, her mind was racing. Why didn't she accept the date this weekend? Was she just waiting to see if Todd would dance with her? She didn't expect him to ask her for a date, but her common sense told her that he was shy and wouldn't ask her to go out until he felt more at ease around her.

She didn't really know why she had turned Darren down. She felt as though she had put the incident behind her, but she also knew she wanted to go to the dance by herself.

Bettie Poole came back into her daughter's room after Denise had finished her conversation. "Everything all right, dear?" she asked.

"Sure!" Denise replied, "He asked if I would go to the dance with him Friday night, but I turned him down. We'll talk to each other when he comes home for Thanksgiving."

Her mother said, "Good, I don't know if you are ready to go out with him at this time."

Denise responded, "Well, he did apologize for what he did."

Her mother was pleased he had realized his actions were not appropriate and that he had been big enough to admit it.

Her mother thought a moment and said, "Dear…don't rush into going out with Darren. Make sure that you are over that incident at the party, and don't go out with him unless you are one hundred percent sure that's what you want to do."

Denise looked at her mother, and asked, "You don't want me to go with him again, do you?"

Her mother smiled and said, "You know how mothers are. Very few boys are worthy to go with their daughters. I want you to be happy in what you do." She hesitated a moment and added, "Denise, I trust you and know that you will make wise decisions."

The young girl looked at her mother and said, "Thanks, Mom, I'll be careful, and I will make the right decisions."

•••••••••●•••••••••

It was a cold November night as Todd arrived at the dance. He had walked rather briskly to get there because the north wind was cutting right through him. He looked back outside and thought, *"At least when I go home, I'll be walking with the wind."*

He turned around and realized that he was rather early. Not many people had arrived. Some of the teachers needed help in setting up a refreshment table and were glad to see him. Todd didn't mind because it made him feel good to help.

As people came in, Todd realized that many of the students were not with dates. Most had just come in small groups. He hoped that Denise would come by herself. It wasn't too long before Clay and Cindy come into the gym.

When Clay saw Todd, he excused himself and walked over to him. He asked, "Has Denise come in yet?"

"Not yet," Todd replied.

Clay continued, "Kim is coming by herself tonight, so you had better be on your toes."

Todd thanked him and again began to look for Denise. It wasn't too long until he noticed her coming in. He was relieved to see that she was by herself.

The disc jockey played several songs before Todd could find the courage to ask Denise for a dance. He wanted to ask her, but every time he started over to her, something would prevent him. Finally, there was a slow song that he thought he could handle, so he asked for a dance.

Denise smiled and said, "Sure, Todd. I would love to."

The couple moved onto the gym floor and started dancing. During the dance, Todd looked up and saw Clay give him a thumbs-up.

Todd felt a little clumsy at first, but Denise was a good dancer and soon had him feeling comfortable about his dancing. She looked Todd in the eyes and said, "You look nice tonight."

He grinned and said, "Thanks, so do you." He wanted to say more, but the words were hard to find. The things he would like to say wouldn't come out of his mouth.

He was enjoying holding her close to him as they danced, and finally commented, "You sure are a good dancer."

Denise again looked him in the eyes and said, "Thank you." Her eyes made Todd feel mushy on the inside. His heart sped up and his knees felt weak. He had read about this happening in stories, but this was real.

The song ended, and Todd wished for another slow number so he could continue the dance. Sure enough, the disc jockey played another song Todd liked, so they stayed on the floor.

Conversation was hard for him because he was so fascinated by being close to a girl that he liked. As they danced, Denise helped him keep the conversation going by asking him about college.

She wondered why he was so shy. He was handsome and athletic. His body was firm, and she could feel his strength as she leaned against him.

Being a woman, Denise found satisfaction in boosting his ego.

The two of them danced several dances together, but Todd didn't feel comfortable dancing the faster numbers, so this gave them the chance to mingle with some of his friends.

Todd found Coach Berry at the refreshment table and visited with him for a few minutes. As the coach and athlete visited, Todd noticed Denise and Mandi were visiting together as they headed toward the restroom.

As Denise and Mandi were coming out of the rest room, Mandi commented about Denise dancing with Todd. Denise assured her that they were just friends, but she did say that she enjoyed dancing with him.

The two girls started across the floor when one of the senior boys stopped Denise and asked her to dance. She smiled and said, "I'd love to."

From the refreshment table, Todd saw the couple dancing. He knew this would be a good time to ask Kim to dance. Kim quickly accepted the invitation, and they made their way to the dance floor. Todd enjoyed the dance with Kim, but his eyes and mind were thinking about Denise and her partner.

As the song ended, Todd thanked Kim and excused himself in order to get closer to Denise. He asked her for the next dance. The couple smiled at each other and wondered what the other was thinking. They stepped onto the dance floor, and Todd put his arms around her and drew their bodies together.

Denise put her head next to Todd's solid body and closed her eyes as they moved smoothly with the music. She felt secure in his strong arms.

The more Denise was around Todd, the more she liked being with him. As the dance ended, she looked into Todd's eyes and asked him, "Would you like a ride home after the dance?"

He was pleasantly surprised at the offer from this attractive girl and quickly replied, "Sure, I would love a ride on a cold night like this." He hoped he didn't sound too eager as he accepted her proposal.

Time passed extremely fast for Todd. This evening had been more than he had dreamed. He wanted it to last forever.

Denise looked at her watch and commented, "It's eleven o'clock; would you like to go for a ride?"

Todd's heart began to pound as he answered, "Sure, let's go." He put on his letterman's jacket and helped Denise into her coat as they started out of the gym. Clay pulled Todd aside and asked, "Are you leaving with Denise?"

Todd responded with a smile, "Yep!"

Clay smiled and joked, "Great! Make sure you go straight home."

Todd laughed with Clay and commented, "I'll call you first thing tomorrow."

Denise led the way to the car. The north wind was cold, so the couple huddled close together as they moved through the parking lot.

Neither of them noticed a white van parked between them and the car. As they walked by it, two hooded men jumped out! One grabbed Denise while the other stuck a gun to Todd's head and snorted, "Get in the car, and don't try to be a hero!"

Todd could see the terror in Denise's eyes and pleaded, "Leave her here! I'll go with you. Just leave her alone!"

The man with the gun said, "Shut up and get in!"

The driver screamed, "Hurry up, somebody's coming!"

The couple was pushed into the back of the van as one of the men jumped in behind them.

One of the teachers, Mr. Thompson, came running towards the van. The driver held a gun out the window and fired off several rounds in the direction of the teacher, who quickly fell to the ground.

The kidnappers sped off as several people came running out the gym door.

The principal, Mr. Black, hollered, "What happened?"

Mr. Thompson replied, "I'm not sure! I think someone was kidnapped!"

Mr. Black yelled at Coach Berry as he came running out of the gym, "Quick!! Call the police! We may have had a kidnapping!"

He then asked, "Who was it?"

Several people began to gather as the teacher said, "I don't know. I didn't get a very good look at them!"

Clay said, "Denise Poole and Todd Perry just left the dance. Do you think it was them?"

Mr. Black quickly said, "See if her car is still here!"

Mandi pointed at Denise's car and replied, "There it is! That's her car!"

The principal went over to check the car and found a note under the windshield wiper. He read the note and frowned as he commented, "Denise has been kidnapped, and the kidnapper will be calling Mr. Poole about a ransom."

Clay was startled when he stated, "They must have taken Todd with them."

Mr. Black asked, "What were they driving?"

Mr. Thompson said, "It was a light-colored van, and the right taillight was broken. That's all I can tell you! "

Mr. Black then asked, "What direction did they go?"

The shaken teacher replied, "They headed north, but who knows for sure if they'll continue in that direction?"

When the kidnappers left, the man in the back, Donald, took a hood and placed it over Denise's head. He then took off his hood and placed it over Todd's head, making sure to turn the eye holes to the back. Neither teenager could see with the hoods over their eyes.

He then tied Denise's hands behind her. As the van turned corners and hit bumps in the road, Donald fell on the victims several times. After tying the girl's hands, he moved over to start on Todd.

Remembering an old Indian trick he read about in one of his frontier stories, Todd flexed his muscles and bent his wrist, hoping to make his wrists as large as possible. He hoped when he relaxed his arms, the ropes binding his wrist would be loose enough to get his hands free.

Donald was having a difficult time securing the ropes as the back of the van bounced and swayed. It seemed to bounce higher with each bump it hit. The old Indian trick seemed to work because the guy that tied his hands kept falling. Being in the dark also helped because the man never realized what Todd was attempting.

When he was through tying the two, he moved to the front with the other kidnappers. The driver, George, told the leader, Sid Smith, "It's a good thing we watched her leave the house tonight. We might not have known which car she was driving."

Sid grinned and replied, "That's right! Planning makes a difference when you pull off something like this."

George asked Sid, "Why did we bring the boy with us? That wasn't in the plans."

He responded, "That's right, but we may need to leave an example somewhere to show Poole that we mean business."

Suddenly, Todd realized what had happened. He thought, "*Man! That guy had a gun pointed at my head.*" He knew he could have been killed. He could still get killed if he didn't watch what he was doing. He told himself, "*Calm down and get control of yourself.*"

He began to wonder what direction they were going. He knew when they crossed the railroad tracks, which meant they were going north. But were they going north, northeast, or northwest? He couldn't tell. One thing was for certain, and he had to choose the right time to try to get loose. Three to one weren't good odds. He kept saying to himself, "*Be calm. Don't do anything foolish. You can't help Denise if you're dead!*"

Todd knew he and Denise were lying in opposite directions, and he quietly whispered, "Denise...Denise...are you okay."

She softly whispered back, "I think so."

He whispered to her, "Just keep touching me so I'll know you're okay."

An irritated Sid turned around and said, "Shut up back there! No talking!"

· · · · · · · · ● · · · · · · · · ·

Many of the students at the dance were shaken and startled about their friends being kidnapped. Several of the girls were crying and tried to understand why someone would do such a thing.

After moving back into the gym to get out of the cold, Mr. Black tried to get as much information as possible before the police arrived. He could see that it was going to be difficult because there was only one witness, and he was badly shaken.

One of the teachers pulled the principal aside and said, "Mr. Black, someone needs to notify the Pooles and Poppy about what happened."

He replied, "That's right! Don't let anyone use the phone until the police get here. At that time, we will go with the officers to tell them!"

In just a few minutes, everyone could hear the sirens screaming up to the gym. As the policemen came in, Mr. Black met them at the door. He told them as best he could how a teacher had seen the kidnapping take place but wasn't able to give anymore details.

When he told them Denise Poole and Todd Perry were missing, the officers became concerned. The officer asked Mr. Black, "Do you think there will be a ransom demand?"

He replied, "It sure looked like that's the intent by the note they left on her car." The principal then told the policemen about the contents of the note as he handed it to the officers.

When he told the police about Mr. Poole having to pay a ransom, they knew that the kidnapping was serious and could be dangerous for the two teenagers.

The police questioned several adults who had been near the door. It soon became obvious that no one had seen what the kidnappers were driving and could only guess they were heading north.

When the police chief arrived at the gym, he asked several questions about the incident. Finally, "Has anyone notified their parents?"

Mr. Black replied, "No sir! We were waiting for you to get here. We wanted you to be with us when we tell them."

The chief then added, "We need to notify them immediately and see if they have any idea who might have done this."

The police quickly went to the home of Mr. and Mrs. Poole. The Pooles were visibly shaken when they were told about the abduction of their daughter.

They sat down in the living room, and it was clear that Mrs. Poole was taking the news rather hard. Mr. Poole asked the police chief if they had any idea about who might have done this.

The chief answered, "We were going to ask you that question. It seems from the note they left, you must have prosecuted one of these guys at one time. He made it clear in the note that he was going to get even with you for putting him in prison. Who have you prosecuted that might make such a threat?"

Don Poole thought a while and said, "There was a young man about six or seven years ago. He made a threat about how he would get even for going to prison, but…what was his name? It seems like… his name was uh…Smith. Yeah! That's it…Smith…Sid Smith. That's his name, Sid Smith."

The chief turned to one of his officers and said, "Find out what you can about Sid Smith. You may have to get some people to come to headquarters or call some people to come to the courthouse. Whatever you have to do, do it and do it now!"

The officer said, "Yes sir!" and left immediately.

The chief then turned around to Mr. Poole and told him, "These guys may ask for a rather large sum of money. We need to get some detectives to come to your house and tap your phones. This may help us locate them."

Don Poole said, "Whatever we need to do, let's do it. Bettie and I will cooperate in any way possible. The sooner we know something about them, the better chance we have of getting Denise and Todd back safely."

The chief responded, "Good! Most kidnappers today probably realize that the phones will be tapped, so they may have some trick up their sleeves. I don't want to waste any more time. Let's get started."

As they were getting up, Mr. Black said, "What about Poppy? You know that he has a heart condition, and this could be dangerous if not handled properly."

The chief said, "That's right. We'll have to be careful."

Several more officers and sheriff's deputies had arrived by this time, and the Chief found two who knew Poppy well. He told them to go to Poppy's house to tell him what had happened to Todd. He warned them to be careful because of his heart condition. As they were leaving, the chief told them, "If he shows any sign of having a problem, call paramedics immediately."

Poppy had already gone to bed when the two officers drove up to his small house. They walked up on the squeaky old porch and calmly knocked on the screen door. It took Poppy several minutes to answer the knock. "What's wrong, officers?" Poppy asked.

One of the officers said, "May we come in, Poppy?"

"Sure, come on in; but something's happened to Todd, hasn't it?" Poppy muttered in a nervous tone.

The officer, not wanting to prolong Poppy's wait, said, "That's right, Poppy…Todd was kidnapped along with Denise Poole about an hour ago. They were leaving the dance when it happened."

Poppy didn't hide his concern as he sat down. The officer continued, "Poppy, he and the girl were okay when they left the dance, and we don't have any reason to think that they might have been harmed since they left. The evidence makes it seem as though there will be a ransom for the Poole girl."

He hesitated a moment and continued, "Poppy, they were there to kidnap Denise Poole, but Todd was with her so they took him, also."

Poppy began to look pale. One of the policemen asked him if he was all right. He commented that he wasn't feeling very good and that he needed his medicine. The policeman looked at his partner and said, "I'll get the medicine, and you call the paramedics." The officers got his medicine and stayed until the ambulance arrived.

The paramedics told the two policemen that with Poppy's history of heart trouble, they needed to take him to the emergency room to play it safe. One of the officers said, "Good, I would feel better if he was in a hospital."

One of the officers leaned over to Poppy as the paramedics were strapping him to the gurney and said, "Poppy, take care of yourself. Todd will be okay. He's smart and won't do anything foolish." Then he assured the old man that they would lock up the house and keep an eye on it until he returned home.

Poppy weakly replied, "Thank you, and I know Todd can take care of himself."

· · · · · · ● · · · · · · ·

The ride in the back of the van had been long and rough. Denise had kept her head against Todd's back most of the time. She tried to figure out what happened and why it happened to her? With her head next to Todd, she thought, "*Why did they have to bring Todd if they were after me? Why did he try to come in my place? He could have been home and safe if he hadn't been with me.*"

She wondered, "*What will they do to me? Will they kill me? Will they rape me? Who knows what they will try?*" Then she wondered, "*What would Todd do if they tried to harm me? What would they do to him?*" She could think of all kinds of questions, but she could never seem to find any answers.

She prayed off and on during the bumpy ride. That was about all she could think of that might help. She sometimes prayed at home and at Christian meetings, but she had never been in a life and death situation before, and she was afraid that she wasn't praying effectively.

Her mind continued to ask, "*Will God hear my prayer? Will He help us get loose? How will I know if He is showing us what to do?*" As the ride got longer and longer, her mind wandered between danger and prayer.

She couldn't keep the tears from forming in her eyes. She had never been this scared in her life. What seemed to scare her most was not having any control of what would happen to her. Todd wouldn't have any more control over the events than she would.

Todd could hear her sniffing, and he knew that she was probably crying. He sensed that she must be miserable, crying and not being able to wipe her eyes or nose. He wished he could put his arms around her and give her comfort, but at this moment, that wasn't possible.

The trip was getting longer and longer, and Todd could hear the men talking about the ransom. As they continued to talk, he heard them talking about making the phone call to the Pooles. The best he could make out was that the guy who had tied them up would be left with the two hostages while the other two men would leave to make the call.

Todd couldn't hear everything, but it sounded as if they would be taken to a cabin and left there until the money could be secured. The trio had not said anything about what they were going to do with their captives, which concerned Todd. He didn't know how much Denise was hearing or how much it was scaring her.

If two of the men were going to make the call about the ransom, that would have to be the time to make his move. He again warned himself to be careful and plan his escape. It would have to be at just the right time.

Todd now tried to visualize what he and Denise would need to take with them when they got loose. He thought, "*Let's see, a cigarette lighter is a must with the weather cold, some kind of a weapon, food, tent or some kind of shelter; and we will have to take our jackets.*"

He tried to memorize what would be needed and told himself to be thorough and wise when they escaped. He tried to think of how the Indians would hide their trails, and he definitely wanted to make sure they couldn't be followed.

He began to plan how he would eliminate the kidnapper. He would first free his hands, then he would have to get the man close enough to slap his ear. He knew that when the eardrum was ruptured with a lot of force, the victim would probably not have any equilibrium. He would have to strike quickly and forcibly.

Todd had never hurt anybody like this before, but this was a life or death situation. He also had Denise to think about. Her life was in his hands, and he felt that with his knowledge of survival, he would be successful in getting them home safely. He tried to remember some survival stories he had read about in his western novels. With the weather getting colder, Todd knew there wouldn't be any room for error.

Suddenly, the van slowed down and the road got rough. Todd knew they had turned onto a dirt road. His heart sped up, and he began to get nervous. He noticed that Denise was not touching him. He immediately moved backwards until he touched her body, and then he heard her whisper, "I'm okay, Todd. I'm okay."

Todd could tell by the conversation of the three men that they couldn't be too far from their destination. The ride had been several hours long. He had no idea what direction they were going or where they might wind up. He wondered how long it had been since the kidnappers had taken them from the school dance.

Denise had slowly calmed down during the trip. It had not been easy, but she kept telling herself that somehow they would get loose. Now, as the van had slowed down, she began to get scared again. She didn't like being a baby, but that thought didn't keep her from crying.

It was several more miles before Todd heard one of the men say, "There it is; I see it!" He knew that the next few hours were going to be critical, and he wanted to rise to the occasion just as he had in several of his football games. He knew that this was not a game; and if he wasn't careful, he and Denise could be killed.

CHAPTER 5

The three gunmen were relieved to get to the cabin. They had pulled off a kidnapping with very little resistance. Outside of being spotted by one of the teachers at the school, they had very few problems. The only change of plans had been bringing two victims instead of one.

They got out of the van after the long ride and went to the back to get the two teenagers. Todd was the closest to the back door, so he was the first one out. He could not tell where they were leading him because of the hood over his head.

Todd was nervous when he got out, but he was also stiff from being cramped in the back of the van. The first thing he did was turn his arms slightly to make the ropes around his wrist look tight.

Denise was the last one out of the vehicle, and she was also stiff. She was so scared she was shaking. She couldn't see because of the hood over her head and didn't know where Todd was. The kidnappers took the two victims and led them to the cabin. Both stumbled on rocks and uneven ground.

Todd could tell by the sound of things that Sid had opened the cabin door while the other two men jerked him and Denise by the arm. This made Todd mad, but he knew that he had to remain calm. This was no time to lose his temper.

They had to step up to reach the porch. As they entered the cabin, there was a musty smell in the air. They were led through the cabin to what must have been a back room. Todd could smell the fumes from an oil lamp Sid lit.

The room where Todd and Denise were placed was cold and dark. They were forced to sit on the floor next to an outside wall. Todd couldn't see with the hood still over his head, but he knew there wasn't any light in the room.

He heard the two kidnappers leave and go to the front with Sid.

Todd wasn't far from Denise, so he scooted until he was next to her. He asked her, "How are you doing?"

Denise replied, "I think I'm okay. I sure was scared when we got here."

Todd said, "I know what you mean. I don't believe I've ever been this scared."

Denise said to him, "Todd, I'm sorry I got you involved in this mess."

He responded, "I'm glad that I am with you. I would hate to think you were here by yourself."

She agreed, "It really would have been scary if I had been kidnapped by myself."

Todd cautioned her, "We have to be calm and do what they tell us. We don't want to do anything foolish."

Denise asked, "Do you have any idea where we are?"

Todd replied, "None whatsoever."

After being alone for several minutes, Donald came into the room to check on the pair. He yelled to Sid, "They look fine. They're just sitting on the floor!"

He then walked over to Denise and mumbled, "Hey, you're good looking, aren't you. Too bad we have to leave that hood over that pretty face."

Denise could feel her skin crawl as he leaned close to her. He had an odor about him that almost made her nauseated.

Todd could feel chill bumps go up his spine. It was all he could do not to say something, but he knew it wouldn't do anything but create problems. It was important not to do anything that would impair their chances of getting free.

Donald made several more harassing comments to Denise. Todd knew she was frightened. He was getting more upset, but just as he started to say something, Sid called Donald back to the other room. As he left he commented, "See you later, sweetie."

Todd could hear Denise groan as Donald left the room. He softly said, "Stay calm, Denise. You handled the situation as best you could. Just don't panic."

She told Todd, "That's the most sickening thing I've ever been through. I thought I was going to throw-up."

He replied, "You handled it very well."

Todd heard Sid say, "We need to get a few hours of sleep before we make that call to Poole." The other two agreed, and the trio finally got quiet.

Todd leaned over to Denise and said, "Try to relax and rest as much as possible. Tomorrow may be a long day."

He was already making plans for their escape, but he didn't tell Denise because he didn't want to take a chance of being heard. He also didn't want to get her hopes up in case something went wrong with his plan.

Denise said to Todd, "I'm cold. Are you?"

He replied, "A little bit." He then moved until they were touching each other. They huddled as close as they could. He felt her shake several times from the chill in the room and knew that she was not only cold, but also scared. Either way, he couldn't help her at this time except by being close. As they leaned against each other, Todd slowly and thoroughly studied his plan for escape.

Morning slowly crept in as Todd and Denise drifted in and out of a light and restless sleep. The driver of the van, George, came into the room and told them he was going to feed them. He raised their hoods just high enough to give them food.

The breakfast of poorly-cooked, hard, stale biscuits wasn't good, but it was food. The young couple ate slowly and forced the food down with cold water. After feeding them, George pulled the hoods down and went back to the other room.

Todd joked to Denise, "Hope your breakfast was better than mine."

Denise commented, "Hardly! I was barely able to swallow it."

The two prisoners could hear Sid as he went over the plans again with George. He told George they would leave shortly to make their phone call. The plan was to use a cellular phone and drive into another calling area to make the call. By going into another area, a different phone tower would be used to transmit the conversation.

Sid reminded his two partners that more than likely, the police would have a tap on the Pooles' phone. The call would be easy to trace, but after they were through making it, they would come back to the cabin. The law would be looking for them in the wrong area. They laughed about how they were going to outsmart the police.

Sid warned Donald, "Watch them close. We don't want anything to happen to them."

Donald replied, "That's right; they are worth a million bucks."

They laughed at the last comment. Sid said, "We'll be back in a couple of hours."

They all walked outside as Donald commented, "Bring us something to eat when you come back. I don't think breakfast is going to last me very long."

Sid smiled and said, "Don't worry! We'll bring something good for lunch."

Todd knew this was going to be his best chance to get loose; he worked quickly to free his hands before Donald came into the room. He took his freed hands and turned the hood around so he could see through the eye-holes. He was relieved to see that it was still fairly dark in the room where he and Denise were staying.

Todd knew Denise would be scared when he made his move, but he wouldn't take a chance of telling her about it.

He had just put his hands behind him when he heard the door to the cabin open. Todd knew Donald was coming back into the house. He made sure he could use his arm in a quick motion.

His heart started to pound as he got ready to act. It was beating so hard his head was hurting. He reminded himself to relax and be ready. If he were to overreact, it could cost him the chance to get free. He didn't know what kind of fighter Donald would be, and he really didn't want to know. He wanted this to be quick and conclusive.

Donald walked into the room and said, "Well, it's just us now."

Denise began to get scared. She wondered, "*What is he going to do? What can I do to protect myself?*"

Todd said to his captor, "Why don't you leave her alone!" He was hoping Donald would come over to him and get close enough for a quick blow to his head.

Denise quickly hollered, "Todd! Be quiet! I'm okay!"

Donald was startled that Todd would say anything. The kidnapper walked over to Todd and snorted, "My, aren't you a brave one!"

Donald wasn't close enough for Todd, so the teenager exclaimed, "You weenie! You're afraid to mess with a man!"

Denise shouted, "Todd! Stop it!"

That last comment made Donald furious. He said, "I'm going to teach you some manners." He bent over to strike his prisoner, when Todd struck as quick as lightning. Todd's open palm caught Donald square on the ear. Donald's head must have felt as if it had exploded. He grabbed it with both hands and quickly fell to the floor.

Denise screamed as Donald went into convulsions on the floor. She was afraid something terrible had happened to Todd. She couldn't figure out what was happening and was about to panic. She felt terror come over her as her imagination ran wild.

Todd jumped up and grabbed Donald and threw him head first into the wall. The kidnapper slumped to the floor unconscious. As Todd looked at his victim, he noticed blood coming out of his left ear. He was relieved to know he didn't have to fight.

He could hear Denise calling his name, and he told her, "I'm okay. We're getting out of here." He quickly went to her, untied the ropes binding her hands, and then helped her to her feet. He gently took the hood from her head and said, "It's okay! It's okay!"

Denise grabbed him and held on as tightly as she could. She buried her head in his chest and asked, "What happened?"

Todd replied, "I'll tell you later! First, let's get him tied up."

Todd made sure he tied Donald securely, then turned to Denise and said, "We don't have much time, so listen carefully! We need to get as many supplies as we can before we leave! First, find a cigarette lighter, then gather what food you can find!"

Todd began to see what else was available for their escape. He found a hand-gun and some ammunition. There were several rifles on a table, so he took one and set it aside. He took the rest of them, cleared the ammunition, and placed them in the potbelly stove. The stove had a good fire in it to keep the front part of the cabin warm and Todd knew it would ruin the guns. Hopefully, Sid and George would not have any weapons with them. This would give Todd an upper hand if the kidnappers tried to come after him.

He noticed several camping items that must have been there in case the kidnappers needed to use them in an escape. There were a small tent, a sleeping bag, a small tarp, and a hunting knife. He also found a nice pair of binoculars and several flashlights.

Denise found several small candles, a blanket and a first aid kit. The two nervous teenagers searched quickly for anything else that might be used for their survival.

They packed the equipment into a back-pack and were ready to leave. Todd told Denise, "When we leave the porch, turn around and walk backwards until we get on some rocks or hard ground. That way they can't tell which footprints are ours. All of the prints will be leading towards the house."

They left walking backwards just as Todd had said. They were careful not to leave any more marks on the ground as they retreated from the cabin. When they reached some rocks, they turned and ran for a large area of trees. For the first time, Todd realized they were going to make good their escape. The couple quickly disappeared into the forest.

· · · · · · · · ● · · · · · · · · · ·

The law enforcement officers had attached the wiretap equipment to the Pooles' telephone. The FBI headed up the team of officers involved in the investigation. There were several agents now taking part. Agent Anderson gave final instructions to Mr. and Mrs. Poole. He told them, "Remember, the longer we keep him on the line, the more information we'll be able to get."

Mr. Poole answered, "Yes sir."

The agent then asked, "Does anyone have any questions?" Nobody responded, so he said, "Now, all we have to do is wait for them to make the next move. This will be one of the hardest things we have to do."

Agent Anderson sat down with the Pooles and commented, "Whatever happens, stay calm. Don't panic or say anything that might cause them to harm the kids."

Mr. Poole asked, "Anything in particular I should ask?"

The agent replied, "Yes, there is. Tell them you won't turn anything over to'em until you've talked to Denise." He continued, "That might make them mad, but that's the only way we can be sure she's okay."

Mr. Poole responded, "What if they make threats to hurt her?"

Mr. Anderson replied, "That's possible, but that is about the only thing we can hold over their head. We must talk to Denise before we do anything else."

Bettie Poole tried to think positively, but the realization of her daughter's abduction was very unsettling. She had cried most of the night, but agents and close friends had helped her get through the long, depressing ordeal.

She couldn't keep from jumping when the phone rang about nine o'clock. Don Poole waited for the agent's signal before he answered the phone. He got the signal and picked up the receiver and weakly said, "Hello."

Darren Hornsby was on the other end and asked, "Mr. Poole, have you heard anything from Denise?"

Mr. Poole sighed and answered, "No Darren, we haven't heard anything yet. We're expecting a call at any time."

Darren told him, "I heard about the kidnapping late last night and just had to call to see if you had any news. Would somebody call me when you know something?"

Mr. Poole replied, "Sure, Darren. I'll have somebody call you when we hear from them."

The process of waiting started all over again. There wasn't much conversation, as everyone was deep in his or her own thoughts. The Pooles found themselves staring at the phone, waiting for it to ring.

Other members of the investigative team visited and drank coffee to pass the time.

About 9:45, the phone rang. Mr. Poole again waited for the signal and finally picked up the receiver. He stuttered, "H...uh...Hello."

On the other end Sid Smith said, "Hey Poole, you recognize me?"

Mr. Poole asked, "Who is this?"

Sid responded, "Don't tell me you don't know who I am."

The nervous father said, "How would I know you? You haven't told me your name?"

Sid replied, "Poole, you know who I am. Think back a few years, maybe that will ring a bell."

Mr. Poole responded, "You're Sid Smith, the one that went to prison for a bank robbery; aren't you?"

Sid said, "That's right, Poole. Now you're going to pay. I need a million dollars, and you've got twenty-four hours to get it."

The startled lawyer asked, "How do you expect me to get that much money?"

Sid commented, "Poole, you won't have any trouble getting that much money. I've been keeping an eye on you for years, and you have a lot more than that."

Don Poole then said, "Before I gather any money, I want to talk to Denise."

Sid snorted, "I'm the one giving the orders here, and you better get the money if you want to see your daughter alive again. Understand?"

Mr. Poole responded, "How do I know you have her, or that she's still alive?...There'll be no money exchanged until I talk to my daughter!"

The kidnapper paused a moment and said, "You can talk to her tomorrow at ten o'clock. At that time I will give you the final instructions on what to do with the money. If there are any problems, I'll tell you where you can find the body of the boy that's with her. Another mess-up, and I'll have to tell you where to find her. Remember Poole, she's awful pretty to have to bury. Twenty-four hours, and don't mess-up. By the way Poole, good luck in tracing this call." Sid was laughing as he ended the conversation.

When they finished the conversation, Mr. Poole hung up the phone. His hand shook as he put it on the hook. The FBI agent came into the room and explained, "He was using a cell phone. We know the area he was calling from, but it is rather large, and he could be just about anywhere in there."

Agent Anderson said, "Get a map, and let's look at the area."

One of the other agents brought a map from the back room. They looked at it when one of them said, "They are going to be either in eastern Oklahoma or western Arkansas."

Mr. Anderson said, "Notify the officials in all of those areas to be on the alert for all light-colored vans, especially ones with broken right taillights!" He then looked at his crew and asked, "Are they smart enough to move to another calling area, or will we find them in the area they called from?"

One of his men commented, "That's just what I was wondering, especially since he made the comment about being traced."

Don Poole told the local police chief, "Someone needs to go tell Poppy about the call."

The chief nodded and said, "I'll go see him. The doctors said he has improved this morning. He needs to know we heard from the kidnappers and we think Todd is okay. We won't tell him the kidnappers want to use him to force our hands."

Mr. Poole told the chief, "Let Poppy know we will do everything we can to get Todd back safely with Denise. We don't want anything to happen to him."

The chief responded, "Don't worry. I'll let Poppy know you're doing everything within your power to get both of them back. We've got to keep him from worrying as much as possible."

• • • • • • • • ● • • • • • • • •

Denise and Todd had been running for several minutes when Denise told Todd, "Wait! I have to rest."

Todd replied, "Okay, let's catch our breath."

Breathing hard as she fell to the ground, Denise asked, "Uh... how did you get free?"

He told her how he had been able to get his hands free and how he had disabled Donald.

Denise told him, "I guess God must have heard my prayer."

Todd was uneasy talking about God at a time like this, so he told her, "Come on! Let's go. We will walk for a while, but we need to keep moving."

Denise asked, "Could we rest a few more minutes?"

Todd said, "Not now." He took her hand and helped her up.

As Denise got up, she put both arms around him and said, "Thank you for getting us free. I was so scared. I didn't know what was going happen to us."

Todd put his arms around Denise and commented, "I was scared, too. I've never been in a situation like this before." They stood there for several moments holding each other. Todd relished his new freedom, but holding Denise was also a treasured moment.

Denise closed her eyes and relaxed for the first time since the abduction.

Todd broke the silence by telling Denise, "We need to keep moving."

Denise asked, "Do you think they might be able to follow us?"

He told her, "I hope not. I've tried to make sure we didn't leave a trail. I don't think they have much to follow. Let's go!"

They continued to move away from the cabin and soon found themselves on top of a large hill. In the distance Todd saw a stream. He told Denise, "See that stream? We'll head for it. We'll need water, and it will lead us away from the cabin."

Denise looked at him and asked, "Do you have any idea what direction we're going?"

Todd thought and said, "Yeah, I think we're going south."

She asked, "How can you tell?"

He pointed to the east and replied, "I believe the sun came up over there, so this has to be south...It looks like the stream is flowing south. That will make it easy to know what direction we're going."

Denise responded, "How do you know the sun came up over there?"

Todd replied, "The morning shadows point to the west."

Denise quietly said to herself, "*I knew that.*"

Before they started down the hill, Todd took the binoculars and checked behind them to make sure they weren't being followed. The trees made it hard for him to see, but on the other hand, it would be hard for someone to see them.

They started toward the distant stream. Todd led the way down the hill. It was easier going down the hill than it had been coming up the other side. He kept telling himself to be careful not to leave any evidence of a trail. He knew if they were captured again, he would be badly beaten or even killed.

Todd began to realize Denise was not in as good physical condition as he was. Still, he pushed her to keep moving. Neither of them said much on the way down the hill. He wanted it that way; it gave him the opportunity to think and stay alert to dangers.

They reached the river after being on the trail for several hours. Denise said, "Todd, I have to rest. I can't go any further."

He knew she was tired, so he told her, "Okay, we'll take a break. You sit down here, and I'll be back shortly."

Todd looked for a tree he could climb. When he found one, he carefully moved up it several feet to take a look through the binoculars. He studied the hill they had come down to see if they had been followed.

Todd knew Sid had probably returned by now and was going to be furious, to say the least.

He didn't see any sign of anyone following them, so he carefully climbed down the tree. He went back to Denise and sat beside her. He asked, "Are you hungry?"

She replied, "I'm starved!"

He checked the back-pack and found some snacks and gave her a small amount. He told her, "We will have to eat small amounts until I feel it's safe enough to hunt."

Denise responded, "I understand."

She looked at Todd for a moment and asked, "Where did you learn these survival skills?"

He thought a while and said, "Well, Dad and I camped a few times, but I learned mostly from books."

Denise responded, "I didn't know you read much."

Todd said, "I love western stories. I read them all the time."

Denise smiled and said, "I sure am glad. Otherwise, we might still be tied up in that cabin."

After eating their snack, Todd looked at his watch and said, "We need to get moving. We'll stay close to the tree line in case somebody is watching."

Denise moaned as Todd helped her up. She was stiff and knew she was going to be sore once they had enough time to rest.

Todd put the back-pack on and picked up the rifle to leave. He told Denise, "Look around. Make sure we're not leaving any signs we've been here."

Denise looked at him and asked, "Do you ever get tired?"

He smiled and answered, "We're both tired. We'll find a place to sleep tonight, but first I want us to get as far from that cabin as possible."

He took her hand and led her out of the trees onto smoother ground where they started another leg of their journey. He wondered what lay ahead for them. Could there be bad weather? What unforeseen dangers would there be? What if they were recaptured by Sid and his gang? He wanted to be alert to anything that could possibly happen.

Denise was seeing a side of Todd she had never seen before. She wasn't sure anyone knew this side of him. At school with his peers, he was shy and generally stayed in the background. Out here in the wilderness, he was a changed person. He was in full control. She liked and admired this side of him.

• • • • • • • ● • • • • • • •

When Sid got out of the van, he knew something was wrong when Donald didn't meet them. He ran into the cabin. He didn't see

Donald when he entered the front door. He hollered, "Donald! Donald! Where are you?" He then heard some groans from the back room.

He ran through the door and found his companion tied up and lying on the floor. There was blood coming from his left ear, and it was apparent that he was in shock.

Sid was furious and started to cuss Donald. He screamed, "Where are they? Where did they go?" He shook Donald as if that would bring him back to his senses.

George snapped at Sid, "Get control of yourself; he's been hurt!" Sid slammed Donald against the floor and went back to the front door. As he stepped outside, he yelled, "George get the guns; we have to go after them."

George found the guns in the stove and shouted to Sid, "They've ruined our guns!" He called Sid over to the heater and pointed to the charred weapons.

George told Sid, "All the weapons have either been taken by those kids, or they destroyed them."

Sid studied the remains of the guns. As he looked at them, he became more upset. He steamed, "We've got to find them, and quick! Let's see which way they went!"

Sid and George stepped outside and started looking around. George told Sid, "I don't see any tracks. All of these tracks are going into the house."

Sid commented, "They must have gone out the back!"

The two kidnappers ran to the back to check for tracks but found nothing. Sid became extremely aggravated. He muttered, "They had to leave a trail somewhere."

George said, "It's like they just disappeared!"

"They couldn't *just* disappear. Where would you have gone if you had escaped?" Sid asked George.

They continued to look around as George answered, "I believe I would have stayed close to the road, because it would take you back to the main road where you could get help."

Sid agreed, "That's what I was thinking. We're going to drive down the road real slow until we find them. Watch for anything that might be a clue to where they might be hiding!"

George hesitated a moment and said, "What about Donald?"

"What about him?" Sid responded, "He started this mess by letting them get loose."

"He's hurting bad! We've got to get him some help!" George exclaimed.

Sid responded, "He deserved everything that happened to him!"

George told Sid, "I'm going to get Donald and put him in the back of the van. We've got to get him to a doctor. Blood coming out his ear like that ain't good."

Sid hesitated a moment and said, "Okay, go get him, but I don't feel sorry for him one bit. He may have cost us a million dollars!"

George went to the cabin to get his partner. Donald was still laying in the floor in a semi-conscious state with dried blood on the floor and caked about his left ear.

George cut the ropes loose and tried to get Donald to his feet, but he couldn't stand up. George then dragged his partner into the front room and took a closer look at him.

Sid was still looking for signs of a trail the young couple might have left.

George hollered, "Sid!! Donald's in bad shape! We've got to get him some help!"

Sid snorted, "He can die for all I care. He just cost us a million dollars! Did you hear that? A million dollars! I ought to shoot him myself and get him out of his misery!"

George dragged Donald to the van and put him in the back. Sid grumbled as they got in, "Watch for any sign of those kids along the road. That's our first priority. They've got to be heading for help. Maybe we can find them before they get there. They couldn't have disappeared!" He started the van, and they drove up the road looking for the escaped couple.

Sid asked George, "If they didn't come this way, which way would they have gone?"

George thought a while and said, "This is the only way to get out. If they went some other way, they may never be found. We're miles from any place."

Sid considered what George had said, and commented, "Good! If we don't find them, we will get out of here as fast as we can. Poole could spend years wondering what happened to his daughter. That'll serve him right for what he did to me."

George frowned and commented, "Yeah, but I had rather have had that million dollars."

Sid looked at his partner and said, "Guess we'll just have to find another way to get it."

CHAPTER 6

Sid and George drove slowly, checking both sides of the road. Several times, George got out of the van to check on something, only to be disappointed.

When they reached the end of the dirt road, Sid said, "We're going back to look again. People don't disappear into thin air."

George asked, "What about Donald?"

Sid snapped, "I told you I don't care what happens to him! He got us in this mess by letting them get loose!"

They turned around and went back to the cabin to search for something they might have missed. Sid told George, "Go up that hill and see if you can find anything that could be a clue as to where they might be. I'll circle the house to see what I can find."

George went up the hill about two hundred yards, weaving back and forth looking for signs of tracks. The ground was hard and didn't yield any evidence of traffic. A broken tree branch caught George's eye, but deer droppings erased any idea that Todd and Denise might have gone that way.

The kidnappers looked for over an hour before deciding that it was useless to continue to search for the escaped pair.

George told Sid, "They're probably too far from here by now for us to catch up with 'em."

Sid snapped, "I'd take the chance if we could find a trail."

George muttered, "We need to get Donald some medical help."

Sid stated, "You'd better come up with a good story about what happened to him before we get him to a doctor."

They took their time as they started back down the road. They continued to look for signs of Todd and Denise on both sides of the road, but again were disappointed.

Sid didn't want to go to a large town or city for fear of being spotted. He decided to find a small, rural clinic. In his mind, chances of being recognized would be considerably less.

They took Donald to a small country clinic that was several miles from the cabin. They arrived at the emergency room just after lunch. They told the doctor Donald had been hit in the head by a wild boar while trying to get him out of a trap.

The doctor examined Donald and told George his eardrum had been ruptured. They would have to take him to a larger facility to treat this type of injury.

George asked the doctor if they could get some pain medicine for him. The doctor went to his supply room and came back with a small package of medicine. He told George, "He needs to get his ear checked. He could lose the hearing in his left side if it is not treated soon."

George took the medication, paid for the doctor's services, and went back to the van where Sid had taken Donald.

George knew Sid wasn't going to a larger hospital in this area. At least he had gotten his ailing partner some medication. This would help relieve some of the discomfort Donald was experiencing until they found a better place.

When they left the clinic, a police car drove up behind them. Sid watched him closely. He knew the police officer had taken a long look at their vehicle.

The policeman radioed for a license check when he saw the light colored van with a broken right taillight. The report came back showing the plates had been stolen. He called for a back-up and tried to get closer to the van.

He knew he had to be careful if he caught them because it would be several minutes before help would arrive.

Sid took the first turn he could find. Looking through his rear-view mirrors, he saw the police car follow them, and he knew they had a problem. He didn't know where they were headed, but he sped up on the rough side street.

The policeman used his radio to keep in touch with his reinforcements. He wanted them to know where to find him and the vehicle he was following.

Sid was furious. He snapped, "I should've killed him and left him at the cabin! Now look at the mess we're in!"

They were bouncing around on the rough road with the law getting closer every second.

Sid yelled, "We don't even have a weapon to defend ourselves. Throw something out the back. Maybe that will slow him down enough for us to get away."

George scrambled to the back of the van and opened the back door. He knew he had to be careful or he could be thrown out the racing van. He released one of the back seats and pushed it out the back towards the police car.

The policeman saw it in time to swerve. The big seat bounced on the road, then hit the side of the car, causing a back window on the passenger side to be shattered.

As the policeman continued to get closer, George got another seat free and threw it out the door. This one caught the right front fender of the patrolman's car and caused it to swerve. The officer got the car back on the road without losing control and continued his chase.

George hollered at Sid, "He's still coming!"

Sid yelled, "Push Donald out. Maybe that will stop him!"

George looked at Sid and snapped, "Are you crazy?"

Sid looked back at George and said, "We're going to get caught if you don't do something!"

Before George could answer, Sid lost control of the van and hit the narrow ditch that was on both sides of the road. The vehicle nosed into the ditch and flipped. Dust flew everywhere. George was thrown out the back. He felt his left leg break when he hit and rolled on the ground.

Sid felt the bones of his face crush as he went face first into the steering wheel. When the van flipped, he was trapped upside down between the seat and the dash. At that moment there were no signs of a fire; however, his first thought was the horror of being burned alive. He was scared and began to panic. The harder he struggled, the tighter he seemed to get wedged. He didn't think help would ever get to him, but finally he heard the door pop. He saw a policeman trying to get the door open.

Sid could hear more sirens driving up to the scene and knew he was trapped. Several officers helped get the door open. It took the lawmen several minutes to get the seat moved and to free Sid from the flipped van. He was relieved there wasn't a fire. He shivered when he thought about burning alive.

Sid was handcuffed with his hands behind him and taken to where George was being treated. George asked, "How's Donald?"

An officer questioned, "Who's Donald?"

George answered, "He was in the back of the van."

Two of the officers ran to the van and found Donald unconscious in the back. They waited until paramedics arrived to get him out.

Sid began to feel the effect of his broken nose and other bruised spots. When the pain started to get worse, he felt nauseated. The agony of the injuries became real when he thought about the accident. He wanted to put his hands on his face, but the handcuffs prevented it. He was miserable.

Donald was put in an ambulance and transported to the local clinic and later to a hospital. He was accompanied by one of the police officers.

George's leg was treated at the local clinic. He was then transferred to a larger medical facility. After being placed in a room, he was questioned by several officers about the stolen license plates. The lawmen also wanted to know why they had tried to evade the police.

Sid was treated and transported to the local jail, pending communication with officers in Texas. He was upset about being placed in jail.

He barked, "Why were you chasing us? We haven't done anything wrong."

The police officer told him, "We were going to stop you and ask about those stolen license plates on your van."

Sid snapped, "What makes you think they're stolen?"

The officer replied, "The officials in Texas told us they're stolen. Besides, they want to question you about a kidnapping."

Sid snapped, "I don't know what you're talking about. We've been up here hunting!"

The officer told him, "You're still going to have to answer questions in Texas."

Sid snapped, "Man, you're setting yourself up for a lawsuit!"

The policeman looked at him in disgust and muttered, "Save it for the judge."

· · · · · · · · · · ● · · · · · · · · · · ·

The sun was setting when Todd stopped, looked at Denise, and said, "We need to find a place to set up camp."

Exhausted, Denise commented, "Finally! I don't think I can take another step."

Todd smiled at her and said, "Maybe we can get some rest tonight."

He suggested that Denise sit down and rest while he looked for a good place to put their tent. He thought, *"The tent is small, but it's all we have."*

He was looking for a sheltered place. Todd didn't want to use a camp-fire tonight because he was afraid it could be seen if Sid and George were following them. The wind was out of the south at the moment, which could still be cold if the temperature was low enough.

He found some large boulders and decided to place the tent next to them. They would give protection from the wind, provided it didn't change during the night.

After he put up the tent, he would gather wood in case the weather turned colder.

Todd set the tent up as Denise handed him some of the equipment. They laughed when it wouldn't fit together properly.

Using common sense and suggestions from Denise, Todd finally got the tent together.

Todd told Denise, "Tonight you take the sleeping bag, and I'll use the blanket."

She replied, "Thank you, I appreciate your kindness."

He told her, "Sleeping on the ground won't be comfortable, but we need to get as much rest as we can. We may have to hike several days to get help."

Denise said, "As tired as I am, I think I'll sleep fine tonight."

After gathering wood, he placed it under some rocks so it would stay dry during the night. He searched the back-pack for food, then placed it in the tent. There wasn't much food to choose from, so he took a small part of it and shared it with Denise.

He told her, "Tomorrow, I'll have to hunt for some food. We are almost out. I wanted to wait another day to fire the rifle, but I don't think we have much choice now."

Denise said, "I'm starved, too, but I won't die before you can kill something for us to eat."

Todd was hungry and would have eaten more, but he knew they had to ration what they had. He looked at what food there was and figured they might have three small meals left. Those meals would not be very adequate.

The young couple sat down and leaned against the surrounding rocks, slowly eating their rationed meal. Denise asked, "Are you going to start a fire?"

Todd answered, "Not tonight. It's too dangerous. If we were being followed, it would lead them straight to us."

Denise looked at Todd and asked, "It's going to be cold tonight, isn't it?"

Todd replied, "I'm afraid so."

The sky had turned cloudy, and the air had a damp chill to it. Todd took a walk down to the stream to look around. He was staring at the water when Denise approached. She watched him as the wind blew his sandy hair and thought how nice he looked, even though he hadn't shaved lately. The more they were together, the more respect she found for him.

She asked, "What are you thinking?"

He thought a moment and said, "I was wondering about how long it'll take us to get out of here and what problems we might have to face before we are able to get help."

They sat down together on the large rock overlooking the stream and listened to the water as it rushed by. Denise was the first to break the silence by saying, "I've always loved the sound of running water. It has a soothing effect."

Todd replied, "It helps me relax."

Denise looked at him and asked, "If you don't mind, I would like to hear about your family."

He looked at the water and uttered, "They were good people. Dad worked for a stock company, and Mother was a teacher. We traveled some in the summer to Colorado. Dad always loved the mountains. We camped a few times, but Mother didn't care for staying outdoors; we usually stayed at a resort. As I look back now, the time we had together was short, but it was quality."

Denise asked, "What happened to them?"

Todd continued, "They were going to a convention in Chicago. The plane was landing in a thunderstorm when it went down. They probably never knew what happened."

Denise leaned on Todd's shoulder and whispered, "I'm sorry. How old were you?"

Todd replied, "Nine years old. It was really a blow for me at that age. I don't know if I'll ever get over that feeling."

Denise could almost feel Todd's pain as he told her how he had lived with aunts and uncles on his mother's side before moving in with Poppy, who was his dad's father.

He continued, "Living with relatives wasn't easy. They had their own families to take care of. Even though they were good to me, I always felt like a stranger in their homes. It wasn't anything they did; I probably didn't have a good attitude about living with them."

He paused to think before going on with his story, "This is the first time I've ever talked to anyone about my parents...nobody ever asked me about them before."

Denise looked at him and asked, "You were proud of them, weren't you?"

Todd replied, "Yeah, I really was. We didn't have many years together, but they were filled with a lot of love...I miss that."

Denise leaned her head on his shoulder again. This gave Todd a feeling in his stomach he had never experienced before. It was a good feeling, and he liked it.

There was a warmth and sincerity about her. She was interested in him and his family. He had enjoyed telling her about his parents. Their memories meant a lot to him, and he never wanted to lose them. He glanced at her and asked, "Tell me about your family."

Denise thought a moment and said, "There's not much to say. Dad went to law school and practiced in Dallas several years, but moved to Wills about ten years ago to become district attorney. Mother...well, Mother is a housewife. She spends a lot of time with social activities and working with the church."

Todd asked, "Your parents do a lot at the church, don't they?"

"Yeah, they sure do. I've been involved with the church all my life," Denise answered.

Todd thought a moment and asked, "Does going to church make a difference in your life?"

Denise wasn't expecting that kind of question. She had to think about her response. Finally, she remarked, "I don't know any other way of living...Yes, I really think it does. I would hate to think about living without God. Have you gone to church much?"

Todd replied, "Not really. I've only gone a few times. I didn't really listen to the preacher when I did go. I get more inspiration at the Christian Athletes meetings than going to church."

Todd felt Denise shiver and knew she was getting cold. He said, "We need to get back to the tent. You're getting cold." He got up and helped Denise to her feet.

She put her arms around him and said, "I feel safe around you. I'm sorry you got involved, but I'm thankful you are with me. I would have never gotten loose if you hadn't been there."

She started to turn loose, but as she did, they looked at each other. It seemed almost like the natural thing to do as they kissed.

It was a warm, sincere kiss. Todd had never been kissed with such feeling. He almost felt himself shiver as they parted. They looked at each other for a moment, then turned and started to the tent.

The sky was getting dark when they got to the campsite. Todd told Denise to take one of the small candles and light it when she was inside. He then took the flashlight and said, "Get in the sleeping bag and warm up. I am going to climb up those rocks and see if I can see some guard lights."

Denise said, "I want to go with you."

Todd replied, "No. You stay here. I don't know how hard it will be to climb to the top. I'll be back shortly."

The climb wasn't as hard as Todd had expected. As he stood on top of the rock, he looked for lights that would give an indication that they were close to getting help. He couldn't find any. He looked in all directions, but to no avail. He had expected to see some somewhere. This concerned him. He now began to wonder how far they would have to go to get rescued.

He eased back down the rocks and slipped into the tent. Denise was in the sleeping bag. He took a blanket he had taken from the cabin and rolled up in it. He knew by the hard ground they wouldn't be very comfortable tonight. They probably weren't going to sleep much at all.

Denise asked, "Find anything?"

Todd replied, "Not a thing."

"What does that mean?" Denise questioned.

He hesitated a moment and said, "It means we may have a long way to go to get out of here."

There was silence for a few moments before Denise mentioned, "I have faith in you. I know you're going to get us out of here."

Todd replied, "I know I will, but what happens if the weather gets bad? We've already had a freeze, and it could get real bad, real quick."

He blew out the candle and tried to go to sleep. He didn't want to worry Denise, but he was concerned about what problems might be ahead of them.

• • • • • • • • • ● • • • • • • • • • •

Todd woke up early to find himself stiff and cold. He didn't get much sleep during the night, but he felt he had rested. He had noticed Denise several times during the night, and she seemed to be restless.

It was cold outside, but Todd decided not to light a fire. He awakened Denise and helped her put on her jacket. He told her, "Sit down and wrap the sleeping bag around you until we're ready to leave."

Denise replied, "It sure is cold this morning."

Todd agreed, "We'll warm up once we get moving."

Denise asked, "Are you as stiff and sore as I am?"

Todd nodded his head and acknowledged, "I'm plenty stiff. That ground was hard."

When they had finished eating, they packed their equipment and started their journey.

The sky was cloudy, and the wind was cold. Denise kept the blanket around her for warmth as they followed the river to the south. Todd wondered how far they would have to go to find help. He didn't want Denise to know he was worried about their safety, so he tried to put it out of his mind.

Throughout the day, Todd took the binoculars and checked for anyone following them. He was becoming confident Sid had not found their trail.

He knew they were low on food, so he decided to hunt. He would like to keep some of the snacks in reserve. He didn't know what he would hunt for, but knew he had to find some food.

Todd felt they had made good time. They had warmed up as the sun got higher in the sky. The sun had broken through the clouds earlier in the morning. They had tried to soak up as much warmth as possible.

•••••••●•••••••

The Pooles had been waiting for a phone call since 9:30 a.m. The longer they waited, the more anxious they became. By noon Bettie Poole began to get upset. "What's happened? Why won't they call?" she asked. The FBI was at the house to trace the call when the kidnappers phoned. They were also growing concerned.

Don Poole asked, "Any idea why Smith hasn't called?"

Agent Anderson replied, "I don't know what this means. I would like to meet with my men and see if they might put together some ideas of what this indicates."

The agents went into a back room to discuss why Sid had not made his ten o'clock phone call. They were in the room for almost an hour trying to come up with some reason for the delay.

Bettie continued to ask questions and cry about her daughter. Agent Anderson came back into the room and told the Pooles and local officers he needed to discuss the situation with them.

Mr. Poole asked, "We want to know why you think Sid has not called. Good or bad...we want to know what's happening to our daughter."

Agent Anderson answered, "That's exactly what we intend to do. First, it might not mean anything. They are using a cell phone, and the battery could have gone dead. They may not be in a calling area, or there could be numerous problems with the phone."

He continued, "Another possibility is the kids could have escaped and Sid is looking for them. In that case, I wish we knew where they were so we could catch them."

The agent looked at the nervous parents and said, "The worst case scenario would be if something has happened to one of the kids and they don't want to make contact until the problem has been solved."

Don Poole commented, "That covers a wide range of possibilities. Anything else?"

Agent Anderson said, "Yes. Sid could be doing this just to torment you."

The worried father agreed, "I wouldn't put it past him to do something like that."

Several phone calls came in during the afternoon. Most of them were from friends asking questions about Denise and Todd. Each time the phone rang, anxiety could be seen in the expressions of the stressed parents.

Several friends came by the house to check on them during the long wait for Sid to call. Darren Hornsby dropped by to see what was happening. He only stayed a few minutes and left in a somber mood.

About 4:20 in the afternoon, Agent Anderson's cell phone rang. A man on the other end asked if he was with the FBI. Mr. Anderson acknowledged that he was.

The Pooles knew by the tone of the conversation that it was about their daughter. Bettie became very tense as the agent continued to talk. After what seemed like an eternity, Mr. Anderson finished the call. He said, "We may have some good news. Three men were captured in Arkansas late yesterday that fit the descriptions of Sid and his men. We're not sure yet. They won't talk to the authorities. They had an accident trying to evade the police, and all three were injured."

Bettie asked, "What about Denise and Todd?"

He replied, "We don't know about that yet. I am going to fly up there and see what I can find out."

Don asked, "May I go with you?"

The agent answered, "No! You need to be here in case they call. Remember, we can't be sure these three men are the kidnappers."

The worried father asked, "Would you let us know as soon as you get any information?"

Agent Anderson smiled and said, "As soon as I know something, I'll let you know."

They shook hands, and the agent went to a car and left immediately.

Don looked at his tormented wife and commented, "We still have a long wait ahead of us. Let's try to think of this as something positive."

Bettie agreed with her husband, and they walked outside together to take in some fresh air.

· · · · · · · ● · · · · · · · · ·

Late in the day, Todd saw some rocks that would make a good campsite. It was sheltered on three sides and had a good place for a campfire.

Todd told Denise, "Set up the tent and gather some dead tree limbs for a camp fire. I'm going to hunt for food."

Denise replied, "Be careful. I'll try to have the tent set up when you get back."

Todd left and disappeared into the woods. Denise thought he was gone a long time before she heard gun shots. She jumped when the sound of the gunfire reached her. The sound seemed to be magnified by the surrounding rocks.

Denise was trying to start a fire when Todd came back with a dead rabbit he had skinned.

She muttered, "Ooh! What is that!"

Todd answered, "A rabbit! I've already skinned it."

She looked at the rabbit and said, "Gross! We have to eat that poor little thing?"

Todd smiled and explained, "It may not taste great, but at least it's food."

Denise groaned, "I don't think I can eat a poor little rabbit."

He replied, "It won't be that bad once it's cooked."

Denise needed help getting the fire started, so Todd recommended she use some grass and small limbs. Shortly, they had a good campfire with the rabbit cooking above it. When the meat was cooked, Todd cut it into smaller pieces and gave part of it to Denise. She turned up her nose, but she knew she had to eat. She looked at it and apologized, "I'm sorry little rabbit."

She slowly took a bite and made a face as she chewed the meat. It wasn't as hard to eat as she had anticipated. In fact, it tasted pretty good.

Todd commented, "A little tough, but it'll do."

After eating, Todd gathered some more wood. The sky was dark, and the heat from the campfire felt good. He hoped Sid and his companions weren't looking for them.

Denise was sitting close to the bright fire when Todd moved closer to her. She smiled at him and said, "The fire feels good."

Todd agreed. She leaned her head on his shoulder and put her hands on his arm. He placed his hand on hers and said, "A campfire at night is soothing. I like to look at the fire and visualize the flames as figures."

Denise said, "When I look at a fire, I think of the flames as being alive."

He liked the feeling of Denise being dependent on him. He had never had this kind of responsibility before, and it made him feel like a real man. As he enjoyed her touching him, the thought of their last kiss entered his mind.

They were quiet for a while when Todd told Denise, "We need to get some sleep tonight. When you go to bed, I'm going to climb up those rocks to check for lights."

She looked at Todd and said, "It's dark up there, so please be careful. The last thing I need is for something to happen to you."

Todd helped her up and kissed her. She had initiated the first kiss, but this time, he kissed her.

He helped her into the tent before he left. With the flashlight secured under his arm, he climbed up the rocks. His climb was tougher than the night before. When Todd reached the top, he saw no lights. This bothered him.

He thought, "How far are we from help?" He wanted to be honest with Denise about their predicament, but he didn't want to alarm her, either. As he climbed down the rocks, he tried to decide how much to tell her.

When he crawled into the tent, Denise asked him if he had seen anything. He had to tell her he hadn't seen any lights. She didn't ask any more questions, but he knew she was getting anxious about getting out of this terrifying ordeal. He turned on his side and settled into a light sleep.

Todd was asleep, wrapped in the blanket, when he was suddenly awakened by sounds outside their tent. He had heard barking and growling earlier in the evening, but he hadn't been worried about it since they seemed so far away from their camp. Now, there was something outside their tent.

He could hear growls getting closer to their tent. He quickly picked up the handgun and made sure it was ready to fire.

Denise woke up alarmed by the sounds and asked, "What's that?"

Todd motioned for her to be quiet.

The sounds were too close for him to feel safe. He opened the tent flap slightly when some wild animal snapped at the opening in the tent. Todd jumped back as the tent shook under the weight of the animal. When it jumped back, Todd stuck the gun out the flap and fired. The animals jumped and raced off into the dark. Todd opened the door and fired several more rounds in the direction of the fleeing animals.

It was all Denise could do not to scream when Todd fired the gun. Each time he shot, she would jump. As quiet returned to the camp-site, Denise asked, "What was that?"

Todd answered, "I don't know, but I think they were wild dogs. They were big whatever they were!"

He slept very little the rest of the night. He noticed that Denise had also tossed and turned several times. He knew she probably wasn't sleeping much either.

He was glad to get started the next day. As they followed the river, three things filled his mind. The first thought was the beautiful companion walking beside him. Her safety was in his hands. He couldn't fail to get her home safely.

The second thing that worried him was the wild animals in their camp during the night. How could he have prevented them from getting so close?

The most perplexing thought was the one that bothered him the most. How long would it take them to find help? How far would they have to hike to get out?

When the young couple stopped late in the day to set up camp and eat, Todd and Denise finished what was left of the rabbit. They had made three small meals out of the little animal. He hoped to get something larger when he hunted later in the day.

Denise had finished eating when Todd walked over to the stream. He noticed it had more rapids than he could remember earlier. He climbed onto a rock that was large enough to extend into the water. He had to be careful because it was wet and slippery.

Denise came up to him and asked, "Anything wrong?"

Todd answered, "No, but the river is dropping. The water is rushing faster and harder than it did further upstream."

Denise carefully climbed onto the wet rock to be with Todd. She questioned, "What does that mean?"

Todd replied, "Nothing, except the hill is getting steeper as the water flows down stream."

He couldn't see how far the rapids reached. He looked at Denise and said, "Well, at least we will be going down hill for awhile. He put his arms around her waist as she leaned against his body. They kissed each other. Each time he kissed her, there was more passion in her kiss. Todd enjoyed her response to his affection and wondered what was going through her mind.

After kissing several times, they stood looking at each other for several moments. As they started to leave, Todd began to wonder if he was falling in love with this beautiful woman. He was experiencing a deep feeling for someone he had not felt since his parents' death. Still, this was different. He couldn't explain the feelings he was experiencing.

Denise looked at her handsome companion and thought how polite and tender this athlete was. The more she was with him, the stronger her feelings grew. Her feelings for Darren had been real, but the attraction to Todd was somehow different. The feelings were much deeper.

When she started down the rock, she felt herself slip. She hit the water in an awkward position and felt pain shoot through her left leg. She knew it was broken.

Todd hollered, "Denise!" As he reached for her, she was washed into the rushing water. He saw her disappear into the rapidly moving water.

CHAPTER 7

As Denise disappeared in the water, Todd jumped off the rock and started running alongside the stream. He could see her head come out of the water and gasp for air. His common sense told him he had to get far enough ahead to catch her when she passed. He knew the water wasn't deep, but it was moving rapidly, which made it extremely dangerous.

His lifesaving skills were going to be important to save her. All of his training had been in a swimming pool. This was rapidly moving water, which would be much different and tricky.

Todd ran around several large rocks and fallen trees before he found a spot he might be able to catch Denise. He quickly worked his way into the cold water. It almost took his breath when he dove into the icy stream. He quickly got to his feet and planted them firmly on the slippery rocks and struggled to stay upright. "Where is she?" he thought. "She has to be coming soon!"

He quickly searched the rapids. He saw her head pop up, but before she could holler for help, she went back under the water. Todd would only have to move slightly to get in front of her.

As she approached, he knew he would only have one chance to grab her. He decided not to take a chance of missing. He would get in front of her as much as he could. He could be knocked off his feet if she was moving too fast, but it was a chance he would take. He watched her closely and moved a little further into the water before bracing himself.

Denise hit him harder than he expected. As he went under the water, he grabbed her with both hands. He struggled to get his feet under him as he held Denise with all his strength. The rapids seemed to get faster as he fought to get up. He finally got his feet on some rocks and raised their heads above the water. He secured his victim in his left arm as he took a lifesaving position. He then fought the rapids with his free arm as they began to move towards the bank.

It was hard to move against the strong current and hold Denise at the same time, but his experience and training was paying off. She had enough strength to hold the strong arm around her, which helped him concentrate on his task.

The stream was cold, and they were both numb. Todd fought the uneven ground and rushing water for several minutes before he could get into the shallow water.

Denise was shaking from the cold water and wincing with the pain of a broken leg. She screamed, "Oh! Easy Todd! My leg…I think it's broken!"

Todd reacted, "Which one?"

She replied, "My left one…ooh! It hurts…Please be careful!"

He thought about his lifesaving skills and first aid training. He would have to be careful taking her out of the water. He didn't know how badly it was broken, so he moved her gently towards the bank.

One of his first fears was shock. He would have to act quickly and treat her with care. He carefully carried her from the stream and looked for a place to put her.

He laid her beside a large log to protect her from the light breeze. He tried not to cause any more pain than possible. He told her, "I'm going to the tent! I'll be right back!"

He sprinted to the tent, which was several hundred yards from where he left Denise. While he was running, his mind was thinking of what he needed for first aid. He knew he would have to splint her leg, treat for shock, and move her back to the camp.

He was breathing hard when he arrived at the tent. He grabbed the blanket, the small tarp, and the first aid kit. Todd then sprinted back to Denise.

When he reached her, he noticed she was getting pale. She was shaking from the cold. As he knelt beside her, she pleaded, "Please help me, Todd! It hurts so bad!" She began to cry on his shoulder as the pain throbbed in her leg.

Since she was sitting up holding on to Todd, he placed the tarp under her and carefully laid her back down. He draped the blanket over her and tucked it under the tarp. Todd knew it would take a while for Denise to warm up since she was so wet. He also knew his sleeping blanket would get wet, but at this moment, that wasn't important. Getting Denise warm was the most pressing issue facing him.

When he had her covered, he told her, "I need to look at your leg."

She sobbed, "Please be careful! It hurts so bad!"

He acknowledged, "I know it does, but I have to see what it looks like!"

He removed the blanket, took the hunting knife, and cut the leg of her pants. Denise's leg had a slight deformation above the ankle.

Todd had been trained in his first aid courses to set broken bones, but he had never worked with a real break before. He told her, "Denise...I'm going to try to set your leg, and it's not going to be pleasant."

Denise cried, "Please, not now, Todd! Not now!"

Todd almost wished she would pass out. That would save her from a great deal of pain. He told her, "We can't wait. Once the swelling sets in, it will be too late. Hold on to something!"

He placed his left hand just below her knee and grabbed her ankle with the right hand. He slowly pulled back on her ankle, making sure it was in a straight line.

Denise screamed in pain, "Stop! Stop it! It hurts, Todd! It hurts!"

The leg hadn't moved yet, so he pulled harder. She screamed and sat up as the bone slipped in place. Todd held it firmly in place until she settled back down. He assured her, "It's okay, Denise! It's okay! Just relax!"

She hollered angrily, "Could you relax if your leg was broken?"

Todd continued to talk to her until the pain began to ease. Shortly, she settled down.

When she finally relaxed, he released his grip on her leg.

"Don't move until I get a splint on it," he cautioned.

With tears streaming down her pale cheeks, she muttered, "Don't worry!"

Todd had to find some straight sticks for splints and something to secure it. He finally found some smooth sticks that must have been weathered by the stream.

Finding something to tie it with wasn't easy. He looked around but couldn't find anything. He decided to take the hunting knife and cut strips from Denise's pants leg.

Todd carefully tightened the splints and secured the leg. After placing the leg on the ground, he sat beside Denise and wiped her face with a damp handkerchief from his back pocket.

He could tell she was still hurting from the setting of her leg. She had stopped crying, but she continued to sniff as he put her head in his lap.

Her tear-filled eyes looked at Todd as she asked, "Now, what? How do we get out of here now?"

He replied, "I don't know. We'll worry about that after I get you back to camp."

She asked, "Getting back to camp is going to hurt, isn't it?"

He nodded, "I'm afraid so, but first, let's rest a few minutes."

Todd sat with her for several moments, running his fingers across her forehead and moving the drying hair from her face. He thought, "*How pretty! Why did this have to happen?*"

He began to feel guilty about the accident. Was he negligent in letting her fall off the rock? Could he have prevented her from getting hurt? These questions began to haunt him as he looked at her.

Finally, he decided it was time to move her back to camp. He thought about how he would move her. He could carry her, but it would be painful, or he could fix a stretcher and drag her back to camp, Indian style.

They discussed the problem, and Denise told Todd, "I think I'd rather have you carry me back. We can get back quicker, and I can warm up by a fire."

Todd agreed and prepared to pick her up. He told her, "This is going to hurt, but try to keep your leg straight."

He heard her groan as he raised her up. She laid her head on his shoulder and put her arms around his neck. As he ascended the hill, he chose his path carefully, trying not to jolt her. She still winced in pain several times.

He was beginning to get tired when he reached the camp. He sat her down outside the tent. He reached inside, grabbed the sleeping bag, and pulled it outside. He sat it beside Denise and said, "I'm going to get some wood for a fire. You need to get out of those wet clothes. When you do, get in the sleeping bag. I'll start the fire when I get back."

He started to leave, but stopped. He asked, "Do you need any help getting undressed?"

"Thank you, but I think I can undress myself!" Denise responded. They looked at each other and smiled.

Todd replied as he left, "Just thought I'd ask."

She struggled to get out of the cold, wet clothes. The pain was almost unbearable, and the cool air against her damp skin made her shiver. She slowly got her clothes off and slipped into the sleeping bag. It felt so good and warm.

For the first time since Todd had pulled her from the rushing waters, she reflected on the accident. She thought, "*I haven't thanked him for saving my life.*"

She couldn't remember much about the terrifying experience. However, the fear of dying was a horror she couldn't get out of her mind. She actually thought she was going to die. She placed both hands over her face and sighed as tears filled her eyes.

Todd returned shortly with wood for a fire. He asked Denise, "How are you feeling?"

She answered, "Okay, under the circumstances."

He started the fire and sat down with her. He said, "When the fire is burning good, I need to go back to the stream to get the first aid kit."

He couldn't stop staring at Denise. His feelings were growing stronger each time he looked at her. He would never forget the panic he felt as he watched her disappear under the water.

When the fire was nice and warm, Todd said, "I'm going to get everything we left by the stream. I won't be gone long."

He returned shortly and put the items beside the tent. He looked in the first aid kit and searched for something to relieve the pain. He told Denise, "There are a few aspirin in the kit. I'll give you two now, but we'll need to limit the few that remain."

After giving her the medication for pain, he thought about food. Denise probably would not feel like eating tonight, but he wanted something for her when she did get hungry.

Todd took his rifle and told Denise, "I'm going hunting. I'll be back as soon as I can. Do you think you will be okay while I'm gone?"

Denise replied, "I think so."

He put the gun under his arm and disappeared into the trees alongside the stream.

Denise felt alone and helpless as she sat beside the blazing fire. She thought, "*Things were hard enough before the accident. Now our future is surrounded with uncertainty. How will Todd ever get me home in this condition?*"

Todd was about to give up finding anything, when he saw several wild turkeys. His heart raced as he stopped and slowly raised his rifle. He chose the bird closest to him and aimed at the base of its neck. He squeezed the trigger, and the head disappeared as the gun recoiled. The other turkeys scattered before he could aim and fire another shot.

He took the prey to the stream and quickly cleaned it. He didn't want to be away from Denise very long, so when the bird was cleaned, he ran back to camp. He felt lucky to have stumbled on the birds. Now, food wouldn't be a worry.

When he arrived at camp, Todd immediately checked on Denise. She was very uncomfortable. He placed the turkey over the fire and sat beside her. The aspirin had not provided much relief from the pain, but it was all they had.

They sat quietly by the fire for several minutes. Todd moved so Denise's head was in his lap. He didn't know what else to do. He had so little to work with. He felt helpless because he didn't know how to relieve the pain in her leg.

Denise finally broke the silence, "Todd, I didn't thank you for saving my life…I thought I was going to die in that water."

Todd responded, "I've never been so scared in my life…I couldn't think of anything except getting you out of those rapids."

Tears began to fill her eyes as she asked, "How are we going to get out of here?"

Todd shook his head, "I don't know. I really don't know. Right now, I wouldn't mind seeing Sid and his gang show up."

· · · · · · • · · · · · · · ·

Agent Anderson arrived at the jail in a small Arkansas town shortly after sunset. He identified himself to the local officers. He then questioned them about information they may have gotten from the three prisoners following their capture.

After discussing the chase and arrest, he was taken to Sid's cell. He noticed the prisoner was developing two black eyes from his broken nose.

The agent and local law officers sat down and started to question the prisoner. It was obvious from the beginning that they wouldn't get any worthwhile information from Sid.

Agent Anderson asked, "What were you doing last Friday night?"

"Hunting, that's all…Hunting!" Sid replied.

"Where were you hunting?"

"In the hills outside of town!"

"Anybody with you?"

"Two friends, Donald and George!"

"Where do you live?"

"Dallas!"

"What time did you leave to come up here?"

"Friday morning, early."

"Can anyone else confirm this?"

"The three of us! Isn't that enough?"

"By any chance, did you happen to stop in Wills last Friday?"

"Why would I want to do that?" Sid replied sarcastically.

"You tell me!"

"Man, you're hinting at something, but I don't know what you're talking about"

The lawmen questioned Sid for about an hour, but couldn't get any evidence about the kidnapping.

Without having any success with Sid, Agent Anderson went to the hospital to visit George. He identified himself and began to question the injured prisoner.

Agent Anderson asked, "Where do you live?"

"Dallas," George answered.

"What were you doing Friday night?"

"Hunting outside of town!"

"Anybody with you?"

"Yeah, Sid and Donald!"

"What time did you leave Dallas to come up here?"

"Around noon!"

"Oh really? Where did you stay?"

"In a cabin several miles off the highway!"

"Did you happen to stop by Wills, Texas on the way?"

"Nope!"

"Are you sure?"

"Why should we stop by that rinky-dink little town?"

"You tell me!"

"What are you getting at?"

Agent Anderson paused a moment and asked, "Know anything about a kidnapping in Wills?"

"What makes you think I would know anything about those kids getting kidnapped?"

The agent's eyebrows raised, "What kids?"

George hesitated, swallowed, and answered, "The ones in the Saturday paper!"

"It wasn't in the paper Saturday!"

George became flushed and restless as the questioning continued. After the prisoner became confused, the questions came faster and faster.

Agent Anderson realized George was breaking down. He paused and asked, "Why did you take those kids?"

George didn't answer.

The agent got up and put his hand on the kidnapper's broken leg and sternly said, "I will ask you one more time," as he began to twist George's foot, "why did you kidnap those kids?"

George winced in pain as he sat up in the bed and shouted, "Oh! It was Sid's idea! We were with him! He planned it all! Stop it! That hurts!"

The agent replied, "That's better! Now where are they?"

George relaxed and answered, "We don't know. They escaped. We couldn't find a trace of them. They just disappeared!"

Agent Anderson asked, "Where were they when they escaped?"

The prisoner answered, "At a cabin in the hills!"

The agent asked George directions to the cabin. The prisoner drew a crude map, showing how to get there.

Agent Anderson left immediately to find a phone and call the Pooles.

It didn't take Mr. Poole long to answer the phone. The lawman told the anxious father, "We've got some good news and bad news about Denise and Todd."

"Are they all right?" Mr. Poole asked.

"That's what we don't know," the agent answered. "They escaped from the kidnappers and didn't leave a trail. I'm going out there now, but won't be able to look for any evidence until morning."

Mr. Poole replied, "I'm leaving right now! I'll be there before sunrise. Is there anything I might bring?"

The lawman answered, "Yeah, bring some unwashed clothes and some of Denise's shoes. We will have some dogs, and that may help them find a trail."

Mr. Poole asked, "Where do I go, and who do I talk to when I get there?"

The FBI agent gave the excited father the necessary information and told him, "Don't rush. We can't do anything until morning. We sure don't need anything to happen to you, so be careful."

Mr. Poole told his wife about the conversation. He said to her, "You need to stay here in case the officers need anything else. I'll call you as soon as I know something."

A friend of the family agreed to go with the anxious father. While Mr. Poole was gathering several items, the friend filled the car with gas. They left a few minutes later for Arkansas.

As the sun rose above the horizon the next morning, Mr. Poole and the law officers gathered at the cabin. The group searched for any possible clue Todd and Denise might have left.

The officers were glad to see the search dogs and immediately had them looking for a trail. It had been several days since the couple had escaped, and the dogs were having a hard time picking up any scents. A few small leads never materialized into a trail. The search group slowly became discouraged as all of their leads failed.

At noon, Agent Anderson called everyone together and said, "I want you to continue to search for a trail that might give us a direction. I'm calling for an air search team to get started. They will have a very large area to cover. Any clue, no matter how small, could make the search area smaller. Keep looking for clues."

· · · · · · · · ● · · · · · · · · ·

The sun came up with a cold mist in the air. Denise hadn't eaten anything since the accident, and Todd wanted her to eat some meat he had warmed. She was pale and weak. Todd rubbed his hand across her forehead and could tell she was running a fever. This scared him. He didn't mention the temperature to Denise because he didn't want to alarm her.

She was able to eat a small portion of the meat. Todd helped her get outside the tent and lay next to the fire. He made her as comfortable as possible. She soon relaxed and closed her eyes, trying to ease the pain.

Todd left Denise, walked out to the stream, and sat down on a rock overlooking the swift moving water. He had never felt anyone else's hurt before. This was a new experience for him. He had known hurt when his parents had been killed, but he had not hurt for another person.

He thought about how much his life had changed over the last few days. Denise was becoming very important to him. He almost wished he had been the one hurt. He didn't like feeling Denise's pain and not be able to help. He started to think about Denise's fever. What if infection was starting in her leg? Could she die? What could he do?

His thoughts began to scare him. He couldn't stand the thought of something happening to Denise. He realized that, without help, she could lose her leg, or even worse, she could die. He had to do something.

For the first time in his life, he thought about God. Todd had heard Coach Berry pray at meetings, but he had never prayed himself. He wondered, *"How do you pray? How do you talk to God?"*

He stared at the moving stream and realized Denise's life was in his hands, but he had done all he could. He looked at the sky. The overcast was breaking, and blue patches could be seen between the gray-white clouds. He mumbled, "God...God, I've never asked you for anything before. I don't know what else to do for Denise."

He paused as he realized he was talking to God, then he continued, "Denise has trusted you and gone to church all of her life. She doesn't deserve to hurt like this. Please, God, help her!"

Todd sat in silence and watched the rapids flow down stream. For the first time in his life, he felt he had to make a commitment to God. He was scared and getting desperate.

He looked into the sky and prayed, "God...if you help me get Denise out of this," he paused a moment to think, then continued, "I will do anything you want me to do...I'll do anything. Just help me take care of her."

Tears slowly filled his eyes as he continued to ask for Denise's safety.

He didn't know how long he stayed by the stream before going back to the camp. He stood staring at Denise, this new part of his life. He wanted so badly to touch her and make her well. He had never felt so helpless in his life.

He sat by the fire and looked at the pale face that was so pretty to him. He thought, *"Please God, you've got to help her. I'll do anything for you!"*

The afternoon sky was clear and crisp. The leaves had been so colorful the past few weeks, but it was getting to be late fall now and they were beginning to cover the ground. Still, this was a beautiful fall afternoon.

Todd sat beside Denise holding her hand. His thoughts turned to his father. How would he have handled a situation like this? He thought about their camping experiences but couldn't see how his father would have done anything differently.

He tried to remember a desperate situation in his western stories. How would the pioneer families have handled this kind of problem? He thought, *"Denise probably would have died in those days."*

In some stories he had read, the cowboy would send his horse for help. He didn't have a horse, so that thought didn't help.

Indians were capable of handling situations like this. He paused as he remembered some of their stories. The Native Americans often used smoke signals to communicate over a long distance. "That's it! Smoke signals!" he shouted.

Denise groaned as she jumped and asked, "What do you mean, smoke signals?"

He replied, "That's how we might get help! We'll use smoke signals! I'll have to get a large fire with a lot of smoke. If the wind doesn't blow, it will get high enough for somebody to see it!"

Denise responded, "You think somebody will really see it?"

He looked at her and said, "I don't care if Sid sees it! We need help."

Todd replied, "This may be a forest that the forestry department watches for fires. They could see it and come to check it out!"

He got up and told Denise, "I'll start gathering wood for the fire, now. I want it big enough to be seen, but I don't want to start a forest fire. I'll build it close to the stream in a clearing!"

He worked on the pile until after dark. He put plenty of freshly fallen leaves in with the wood. He hoped they would create a lot of smoke.

When he finished the stack of wood, he went back to their campfire, warmed some meat, and sat down beside Denise. He helped her eat a small portion. Todd wanted her to eat more but didn't force the issue.

Her fever seemed to be getting higher. All he could do was stay close to her and give her as much encouragement as possible.

His prayer was, *"Please God, let somebody see our smoke tomorrow. Help someone find us."* He prayed this prayer over and over. At least now he had hope of getting rescued.

During a restless night, Todd thought about his commitment to God and the idea of the smoke signals. Did God help him come up with that idea? That was a question he would probably never be able to answer.

He had made a promise, and he knew he couldn't let it go unattended. He would follow through with his commitment. But how would he know what God had planned for him? How would he know?

Todd had never been a Christian. He didn't understand how prayer was answered. He didn't know how to listen to God. He was totally confused. Hopefully he would know when the time came.

He wished Coach Berry was with him. He had a lot of questions to ask his coach.

He thought about talking to Denise, but he didn't want to disturb her. He wanted her to rest as much as possible.

Todd was glad when the sky began to turn to light. He didn't rest much between thinking about Denise and his commitment to God. He crawled out of the tent and checked the weather. The air was cold and damp, just like the day before. Best of all, there was no wind. As soon as the sky cleared, he would start the fire.

He carved some of the meat from the turkey, warmed it over the camp-fire and fed Denise. He thought she looked worse. She was still running a fever.

He knew she could get dehydrated if he didn't give her plenty of water. That was something Poppy preached to Todd when he was sick, "You have to drink plenty of water!"

Todd had two aspirin left in the first aid kit. He decided to hold them for an emergency, hoping there wouldn't be one.

The sky slowly cleared, and Todd knew it was time to light the fire. He gathered some of the damp leaves for more smoke and placed them on top. He took the cigarette lighter, lit the grass at the base of the wood, and watched the smoke turn to flames. The fire grew bigger and bigger. He stared at the smoke as it rose.

He prayed again, "Please, let someone see this smoke! Please, God, hear this prayer!"

The smoke was now reaching into the sky. Todd didn't want to take any chances of missing a rescue, so he started building another stack of wood, grass and leaves. He wanted to keep smoke rising as long as possible.

Later, he stopped gathering wood to take a break. He stood by the smoking fire, threw on more damp leaves, and watched the smoke rise. The column stretched into the clear sky. He thought, "Surely someone will see this and come to our rescue. This must be the day."

He went to Denise, sat beside her and prayed quietly, "Please let someone see our signal."

CHAPTER 8

The morning sky was getting brighter as Agent Anderson gathered a small search group. Four pilots had volunteered to fly over the hills in search of Todd and Denise. They discussed the procedures to follow in order to cover a large area of forest.

The FBI agent noted, "We need to search an area that has a radius of approximately 10 to 20 miles." He pointed to a map and continued, "We don't think they have gone east. There are several roads within a few miles, and someone would have seen them. If they had gone north, there are several small towns close to the cabin, and they would have shown up somewhere. So, we want to concentrate on an area south and west of the cabin. That covers an area of 400 to 600 square miles. That's a large area. Are there any questions?"

Seth Hensen said, "I hunt the area along the river, so I'd like to take that zone."

The other three pilots chose an area with which they were acquainted.

Seth asked, "Any idea how far they may have gone since their escape?"

Agent Anderson answered, "We don't really know. If they haven't encountered any problems, they could have traveled ten to fifteen miles."

A local law officer instructed, "When you spot them, radio their location to the base; we have a helicopter and crew on stand-by. We will dispatch them when we get your call."

The pilots went over last minute details and departed for their planes.

Mr. Poole felt helpless as he watched the pilots go to their planes and get ready for take-off. He asked Agent Anderson, "Since we're having to search over a forest, what will be our chances of finding them?"

The agent answered, "I don't know. These men are good pilots, and they know the area very well. If those kids are out there, I believe these people can find them."

The two men watched as the pilots checked their planes for flight. One by one, they climbed into their single engine planes, buckled their seat belts, and went over their checklist. One of the pilots shouted, "Clear!" The engine started to crank, and then it roared white smoke as the propeller began to spin.

As each plane began to start, it moved to the end of the runway. The first plane turned into the wind and began to gain speed. One by one, each nosed into the air. Seth was the third plane into the air. He tipped his wings and disappeared to the south toward the area of the river.

••••••••••●•••••••••

Todd was watching his second stack of wood burn as he sat beside Denise. He commented, "I was hoping somebody would have been here by now."

Denise asked, "Do you really think somebody will find us?"

"I sure do!" Todd replied, "They may not have had enough time to get here."

Denise commented, "You've burned two stacks of wood, and nobody's come."

Todd paused a moment, then uttered, "They will!"

Denise showed an expression of pain as she moved to get comfortable. She looked at Todd and said, "I wish they would hurry. My leg is hurting."

Denise's pain was beginning to bother Todd, so he got up and said, "I'm going to start another pile of wood. There's not much left around here, so I'm going to move up stream to find some."

Denise asked, "How long will you be gone?"

"I don't know. Just long enough to build another fire. I need to hurry because the wind is beginning to blow."

He left the camp and went up stream, where he started to stack more wood. He was having difficulty finding enough dead firewood in the clearing, so he went into the trees to find some.

His pile was getting large, but he decided to make another trip into the trees. As he searched for dead tree limbs, his concentration was broken by the sound of an airplane.

When he realized what the sound was, he dropped his load and sprinted into the clearing. The airplane was just passing overhead when he entered the opening.

Todd shouted, "Hey! We're down here!"

He quickly took Denise's hand mirror from his pocket and started to flash the sunlight towards the small plane. It was too late. The pilot had already passed.

Todd stopped flashing the mirror and dropped his hands to his side. He felt sick at his stomach when he realized he had missed the plane. He thought, "If I had only been in the opening, he might have seen me. What will be the chances of him coming back?"

Seth was flying down the river watching the clearing on both sides of the water. He thought, "I'll have to be careful. Watching the ground go by almost makes me dizzy."

Suddenly, he noticed smoke. He almost missed seeing it as he flew past. He decided to circle back and check for the spot of the fire. The wind was beginning to blow and the smoke was starting to stretch out over the trees. He wanted to find the fire's source.

Todd heard the plane as it began to circle around. He sprinted downstream to his fire that was now burning low. He got the mirror and started to flash the sunlight toward the circling plane. He prayed, "Please God, let him see my signal. Please!"

Denise hollered at Todd, "Did he see us?"

"Not yet, but I think he's coming back!"

Seth circled around and dropped lower to get a closer look. Suddenly, light started flashing in his face. He knew he had found something. As he flew closer to the river, he could see someone flashing signals. Seth tipped his wing to show he had spotted him.

Todd shouted to Denise, "He sees us! He sees us!"

Denise put her hands to her face and fought back the tears of joy. She asked Todd, "Can he land and pick us up?"

He replied, "No, but he can let somebody know where we are!"

Todd stood in the clearing by the stream as Seth circled back. He flew down the stream for one more look. Todd was waving both arms in the air as the plane flew overhead.

Seth radioed the base, "Hello, base, do you read me? Over!"

"This is base; go ahead! Over!"

"I've spotted a young man! He's about nine miles south of the cabin along the river where Beaver Rapids start! Do you copy? Over."

"Roger! You've spotted a young man! What about the girl? Over!"

"Negative! He's the only one I see! Over!"

Mr. Poole heard the excited pilot report finding a young man. He immediately moved closer to the radio to follow the conversation.

The base called back, "Would you repeat how many people you see? Over!"

Seth responded, "One! A young man. He's marked his location with fire that's putting out a lot of smoke! Over!"

"Go back to see if there's a girl with him. Over!"

"Roger!"

The base operator immediately called a waiting rescue team and told them a young man had been spotted along the river. He could be located approximately nine miles south of the cabin where Beaver Rapids start. He had used smoke to mark his location beside the stream.

When they received the call, the rescue team ran to their helicopter and made preparations for take-off. The big overhead blades began to rotate. Dust engulfed the pad as the blades whirled fast enough to lift the helicopter off the ground. As it left the pad, it turned to the south and disappeared over the trees.

Seth circled back to see if there was someone else with the young man who was still waving his arms at the airplane.

Todd heard the plane coming again and waved at the pilot. It was a relief to know they had been found.

The pilot reported, "Base! This is Seth! There's no female in sight! Over!"

Don Poole was listening to the conversation and was getting anxious. He asked the radio operator, "Please, ask him take another look."

The radio operator called Seth, "Circle back and look for a girl that might be at the site. We've just dispatched a rescue helicopter. They should be arriving at the scene in approximately fifteen to twenty minutes. You'll need to be on the lookout for the chopper. Over!"

"Roger!" Seth acknowledged.

The small plane circled back and made one more pass over the rescue area, but Denise was at the camp in the trees, and Seth was unable to see her.

After circling the area again, he reported, "Hello base. There's no other person in sight. Repeat! No girl! Over!"

"Copy!...No girl! Over!"

Seth reported, "Affirmative!"

Mr. Poole sat down and told Agent Anderson, "She has to be with him! Do you think she could be hurt?"

Agent Anderson responded, "I don't know. However, we should know something when the chopper gets there."

The nervous father walked to a window, put his hands in his pockets and commented, "Not knowing why Denise isn't with Todd is killing me."

Don Poole stared out the window for several minutes worrying about his daughter, then sat down next to the radio operator. As the rescue helicopter approached the campsite, the base operator listened to the conversation between Seth and the rescue squad.

The pilot of the helicopter then reported, "Base this is Rescue One! I see the smoke, and I'm preparing to set down. Over!"

"Roger! Copy!"

Todd was beside Denise as the dust circled their camp. Todd and Denise had never heard popping helicopter blades that sounded so good. Just as the chopper touched the ground, two men jumped out of the green aircraft and ran to the couple.

As the pilot turned the engine off, the noise of the whirling blades began to fade. Todd told the rescue team, "Her leg is broken! You'll have to be careful when you move her."

One of the men ran back to the aircraft and reported a female with a broken leg. The pilot called the base to report, "We have an injured female with the young man! Do you copy?"

"Roger! Copy! Young man and injured female!"

The operator replied, "Stand-by for further instructions on nearest hospital!"

"Roger!"

Mr. Poole was greatly relieved to know Denise was with Todd. He sat down, took a deep breath, and relaxed for the first time in several hours.

The rescue team was quickly told, "Transport victim to the county hospital at Smytheville southwest of your location. I'm notifying immediately. Please advise me of your ETA! Over!"

"Copy! ETA twenty minutes! Over!"

"Roger! Copy! ETA twenty minutes! Over!" the base operator responded.

The crew got a stretcher and took it to Denise. They replaced the wooden splints with an air cast. Todd told them he was concerned about her fever. The team leader reassured Todd, "Don't worry. We'll start an IV and have her at the hospital in a few minutes."

They strapped Denise to the stretcher and carefully moved her to the waiting helicopter. They were now prepared to airlift Denise from the area.

Todd retrieved a few items from the tent, snuffed out the campfire and went to the helicopter. He asked them about the fires he had started. They all agreed they should put out the remaining fires before they left. Within a few minutes, they were buckling themselves into the chopper.

As the aircraft lifted off the ground, Todd had never felt such a relief. He took Denise's hand and told her, "Now we can get your leg set right."

Denise replied, "Todd, you have taken very good care of me. You did the best you could."

While they were in route to the hospital, Todd stared at Denise and wondered about what the future would hold for them.

He thought, "*Will Denise still have strong feelings for me once she gets home? How will this experience affect her?*"

He knew their relationship would now be different. He didn't know if that would be good or bad for him. He knew his feelings toward her were much stronger than before the kidnapping.

Denise looked at Todd and thought, "*How thankful I am that Todd thought about starting a fire.*" She closed her eyes and wondered, "*What will happen to us now? Will Todd change when we get home?*"

Denise couldn't answer the questions that filled her mind, but she knew she would always have a special feeling for Todd. She would never forget how he had saved her life several times over the past few days, but she didn't want her feelings of obligation to Todd to dictate what kind of future relationship they might share.

·········●···········

After talking to his relieved wife about the rescue, Don Poole got into the waiting airplane of Seth Hensen. Don's friend who had accompanied him to Arkansas would drive the Poole's car to the hospital. Mr. Poole told him, "I'll be at the hospital in a few minutes. You take your time."

His friend responded, "Okay! I hope Denise is going to be all right."

Don Poole replied, "Thanks! I'm sure she's in good hands by now."

Seth gave the plane power, and it started to move towards the north end of the airport. They slowly gained speed. When the plane reached flying speed, they felt it leave the bumpy runway and climb smoothly into the cool autumn air.

When they landed at a small airport, a police car met them. As Don got out of the plane, he asked Seth, "How can I thank you for finding my daughter?"

Seth responded, "You don't have to. I'm just thankful I was able to spot them. I do hope they're okay."

Mr. Poole replied, "Thanks to you. I'm sure they will be!"

He said good-bye to his new friend and jogged to the waiting car. He turned and waved to Seth as the pilot taxied for a take-off. The pilot returned his wave and started to move down the runway.

When Mr. Poole arrived at the hospital, Todd was waiting at the door. He had only met Denise's father one time, but he recognized him immediately.

Todd was glad to see him get out of the car. The anxious father recognized Todd and quickly went to him and asked, "How is she?"

Todd replied, "She has a broken leg and is running a fever. She is being x-rayed at this moment."

"How bad is it?"

"I think it is a clean break, but we won't know until after the doctor reads the x-ray."

"How did it happen?"

"She slipped off a rock and fell in the river."

"Were you with her?"

"Yes sir! I got her out."

The relieved father responded, "Thank goodness! Are you okay?"

"Yes sir! I'm fine!"

"Can you take me to her?" Don asked.

As Todd moved towards the door, he said, "Yes sir! This way."

They waited at the door of the x-ray room until the doctor came out. When the Doctor looked at Mr. Poole, he asked, "Are you Denise's father?"

He replied, "Yes, I'm Don Poole."

They shook hands as the doctor led them to some chairs. When they sat down, Mr. Poole asked, "How is she?"

The doctor replied, "Her leg is broken above the ankle. It's a fairly clean break, but it will require surgery to set it properly. She also has an infection. We would like to start her on antibiotics with your approval."

Mr. Poole responded, "Sure, as soon as possible. What about the operation?"

The doctor said, "We'll need to move her to a larger hospital to do the surgery. Since she will have to be moved, do you have a preference to where we send her?"

Mr. Poole thought a moment and answered, "Yes! I would like to transfer her to Dallas."

The doctor said, "That's fine, but we will need to fly her there."

"Sure, that won't be a problem. When may I see her?"

The physician said, "Follow me."

Mr. Poole followed the doctor into the x-ray room where Denise was lying on a table. She looked pale and weak as he walked closer to her.

Denise opened her eyes and saw her father standing beside her. She muttered, "Dad!"

He bent down as his daughter weakly put her arms around his neck and held him for several minutes. She cried, "I missed you so much."

As Denise held to her father, he whispered, "I'm so sorry. You didn't deserve this. I wish Sid had kidnapped me instead of you. I'm so glad we have you back."

Todd leaned against the hospital wall and watched as father and daughter held each other. He longed for someone to touch him and make him feel loved.

When Denise finally released her hold on her father, she looked at him and said, "Dad, I don't think I could have made it if Todd hadn't been with me. He saved my life and took care of me."

Mr. Poole looked at Todd and asked, "How can I thank you?"

Todd replied, "I'm just thankful I was able to help her." He wanted to tell this relieved father how special Denise was, but the words wouldn't come out of his mouth. He thought, "*Maybe this isn't the time to discuss my feelings.*"

The doctor asked Don Poole, "Could you come with me, please? We need to discuss moving your daughter while the law officers question her and Todd."

"Sure," Mr. Poole replied.

They went to the doctor's office and discussed plans to move Denise. They decided to transport her by ambulance to the airport where a plane from Little Rock would fly the small group to Dallas.

The doctor told Mr. Poole, "I'll notify the hospital in Dallas to be ready for you."

After Todd and Denise told their story to the officers, they prepared to leave the hospital. Mr. Poole thanked the law officers and the doctor for their help in the rescue.

Since it would be several hours before the doctor would have Denise ready to travel, Don Poole, his friend and Todd went to a restaurant to eat. While they were eating, Todd told them the story of the kidnapping, escape and the injury to Denise.

Mr. Poole told Todd, "I'm thankful you were with Denise and were able to get away from Sid and his gang; however, I'm sorry you had to be subjected to that kind of treatment."

Todd replied, "I'm glad I could help. I don't know what they would have done to her if she had been alone."

Mr. Poole shook his head and muttered, "I don't want to think about that!"

Denise was sleeping when the three men returned to the hospital. They quietly sat down in her room to wait for the airplane. Todd looked at her and thought about how peaceful she looked. He was so thankful they had survived the harrowing ordeal.

When the group arrived at the airport, they could see the plane making its approach for the landing. Mr. Poole told his friend, "You can start back when you are ready. Todd and I will stay with Denise on the plane."

They shook hands, and the friend left for his long trip home.

Mr. Poole and Todd watched as the paramedics placed Denise in the plane. When she was secured, the two men climbed into the plane, buckled themselves to their seats and waited for takeoff. The plane taxied onto the runway, turned into the wind, and picked up speed. Slowly and smoothly, it rose into the November sky.

When the plane landed in Dallas, Mrs. Poole quickly came out to meet the returning group. She could hardly wait to see her injured daughter. She held her right hand to her mouth as Denise was being prepared for transfer from the plane to a waiting ambulance.

Coach Berry had followed Mrs. Poole and a close friend to the airport to check on Todd. He knew he would have to be the one to tell him about Poppy's heart attack. The coach was aware that Todd would be by himself, and he wanted to be there to help his former quarterback.

When Todd got off the plane, he was happy to see his coach waiting for him. He had questions to ask, but he wanted to wait for the right opportunity. At the moment he was glad to see a close friend.

Coach Berry met Todd and shook his hand. He put his hand on the athlete's strong shoulder and asked, "Todd, are you okay?"

Todd looked at his coach and answered, "Yes sir! I'm tired, but glad to be home."

The two stepped away from the plane as the ambulance backed closer to pick up Denise. They didn't say much as she was transferred from the plane. As Coach Berry watched, he knew Todd had developed strong feelings for Denise. He asked, "Would you like to ride to the hospital with me?"

Todd replied, "Yes sir!"

When the ambulance left with Denise, Coach Berry and Todd walked to the coach's car. Todd paused before getting in and asked, "Where's Poppy? I thought he might be here?"

The coach answered, "I was going to tell you later. Poppy had another heart attack the night you were kidnapped. He's in the hospital but should be released in a few days. We'll stop and see him when we start home."

Todd was surprised and asked, "How bad was it?"

"Fairly severe, but the paramedics got him to the hospital quick enough to save his life."

"Will he be okay?"

"I think so. I visited with him yesterday, and he's ready to go home."

"Good! I would like to see him as soon as possible."

Coach Berry said, "When everything is okay with Denise, I'll take you to see him."

Todd replied, "Thanks!"

Upon arriving at the hospital, Don Poole gave the attending doctor the x-rays and information from the Arkansas hospital. After Denise was admitted and taken to a room, Todd told her about Poppy. He told her, "I hate to leave you, but I need to check on him."

Denise said, "I understand. Mother and Dad are with me, so I'm okay."

Without thinking, Denise put her arms around Todd's neck and held him tightly. She whispered, "Thank you, Todd. I'll miss you."

Todd was silent for a moment and responded, "Yeah, I'm going to miss you, too."

He didn't look back as he left. He felt as though he was leaving part of himself in the hospital room.

Denise watched Todd until he was out of sight. She couldn't keep the tears from forming in her eyes. She was going to miss his companionship.

Mrs. Poole took Denise's hand, looked at her daughter and commented, "He's become special to you, hasn't he?"

Denise knew her mother was reading her mind. She never could hide her feelings from her mother. She paused before she answered, "Yes ma'am. He really has."

As Todd and Coach Berry drove out of the parking lot, Todd had so many questions he wanted to ask that he didn't know where to begin. "Coach," he paused then continued, "Coach, how can you tell what God wants you to do?"

The coach gave Todd a puzzled look, then asked, "What do you mean?"

Todd told him about the commitment he made to God after Denise had broken her leg.

Coach Berry hesitated before commenting, "Todd, different people know in different ways. You will know God's plan when the time is right."

Todd asked, "Can you hear Him talk to you?"

The coach replied, "I don't hear an audible voice. But I have a feeling when He's trying to tell me something."

Todd paused before continuing, "I feel like He gave me the idea about the smoke signals, but I can't tell you how I knew."

The coach said, "He always lets us know somehow."

Todd said, "Coach, I was so scared when Denise got hurt. In fact, I have never been so afraid in my whole life. I didn't know where else to turn."

Coach Berry responded, "I can understand. I think you turned to the right source. Todd, would you like to go to church with me Sunday."

Todd replied, "Yes sir! I sure would."

The two continued to discuss the feelings Todd was having when they arrived at the hospital to see Poppy.

Before they got out of the car, Coach Berry told Todd, "Don't hesitate to call me if you ever need help. I'll help you in any way I can."

Todd smiled and said, "Thanks, Coach. I'll remember that."

CHAPTER 9

Todd knocked on the door of Poppy's hospital room and waited for him to answer. The old man mumbled, "Come on in!"

Todd and Coach Berry opened the door and walked toward Poppy. When the grandfather saw Todd, he smiled and said, "Come here, son!" He grabbed Todd and hugged him with all his strength. As he held his grandson, he exclaimed, "Boy! Am I glad to see you!"

He released his bear hug on Todd and asked, "When did you get back?"

Todd answered, "A few hours ago."

"Where's the girl?"

"She's in the hospital in Dallas!"

"What's wrong with her?"

"She fell in a river and broke her leg!"

"Very bad?"

"She's going to have surgery tomorrow morning to have it set."

Poppy hesitated a moment and said, "Sure hope she's okay!"

The young man looked at his grandfather and agreed, "Yeah! Me, too!"

Todd told Poppy the story about the kidnapping, escape, and rescue. The old man listened intently to the story.

When Todd finished telling it, his grandfather commented, "I'm sure proud of you, son. You seem to have used your head."

Todd thanked him and asked how he was feeling.

Poppy snapped, "Should've been outta here several days ago! They say I might get to go home in a couple of days."

Todd replied, "Good! I'll have everything ready for you when you get to come home."

When they had finished their visit, Todd and Coach Berry said good-bye to the recuperating grandfather and left for home.

As they were leaving the hospital, Coach Berry commented, "Todd, since you're back, he won't stay here much longer. He's ready to go home now!"

Todd agreed and said, "I feel closer to Poppy now than I did before I was kidnapped. I guess going through something like that kidnapping makes you appreciate what you have."

While driving to Poppy's house, Coach Berry asked Todd, "Why don't you stay at my house tonight? You're going to be lonesome by yourself, and you're welcome to stay with Beth and me."

"Thanks Coach, but I'm looking forward to being alone and sleeping in my own bed. I'll have to leave early to go to the hospital."

Coach Berry asked, "How are you getting to the hospital?"

Todd replied, "I don't know."

Coach asked him, "Do you need me to take you?"

Todd was relieved his coach had offered. He answered, "Yes sir. Do you mind?"

His coach replied, "I'd be glad to take you!" Coach Berry then asked, "Are you sure you want to stay by yourself tonight? You're welcome to stay with us until Poppy gets released."

Todd assured him he wanted to sleep at home.

When they finally arrived at Poppy's house, Todd got out of the car. Coach Berry stuck his hand out. As Todd shook his hand, the coach said, "Seriously Todd, call me if you change your mind. You may decide that you would like to be with someone tonight. If you do, feel free to phone me, and I'll come pick you up."

Todd replied, "Thanks Coach! I will."

He got out of the car and walked slowly to the front door. Today, he had a strange feeling as he opened the screen and unlocked the wooden door. As he entered the cold, dark room, he experienced a loneliness about the house. So many times he had taken Poppy for granted.

He walked through the house as if he would find something. He knew it had been empty since Poppy's heart attack. However, he hadn't felt this lonely since his parents had been killed.

He thought, "I need to light the heater. Maybe that will warm-up the place."

Todd got the matches and knelt beside the old space heater. He struck a match, turned on the gas, and watched as the flames spread their warmth.

As he got to his feet, he noticed a western novel lying on the table beside his favorite chair. He picked it up, thumbed through it, and laid it back on the table. He thought about how much some of the western stories had helped him and Denise survive a week in the wilderness.

He walked to the heater, turned his back to it and thought, "Why am I so lonely? Is it because Poppy's not here, or—?"

His thoughts stopped for a moment. Was he missing Denise? Her companionship had become very important to him.

His thoughts scared him when he thought about what could have happened to her. He was so thankful Denise was in the hospital and in good hands. He finally admitted to himself that he was beginning to miss her friendship.

Suddenly he was brought back to the present when he heard a car door slam. He looked out a window and saw Clay coming to the front door.

When Todd opened the door, his friend grabbed him in a bear hug and said, "Man, am I glad to see you! When I realized you and Denise had been kidnapped, I thought you might be going to that big stadium in the sky!"

Todd smiled, "Thanks, Clay. You really had a lot of faith in me, didn't you?"

Clay looked at Todd and said, "Bud, it sure is good to have you back!"

Todd admitted, "It's great to be home!"

"How's Denise?"

"She's going to have surgery tomorrow."

"Are you going to be there?"

"Coach Berry offered to take me!"

"Let me take you! Tomorrow is Saturday, and we don't have school. I'd be glad to drive you there."

"Sure, I'd like that. It would mean a lot to me. I need to call Coach and tell him you've offered to take me."

Todd called Coach Berry, "Coach, Clay is with me now, and he'd like to take me to the hospital tomorrow. Is that all right with you?"

Coach Berry answered, "That would be fine, Todd. It'll be good for you two to be together. Hope everything goes well with the surgery, and call me if you need anything."

Todd replied, "Thanks, Coach. I will!"

He turned to Clay and said, "That'll be fine with Coach!"

He continued, "Sit down, Clay! What's happened at school since I've been gone?"

"Not much! The basketball team won their first game last week. Other than you and Denise being gone, very little has happened." Clay paused before asking, "Are you going to play basketball?"

"I don't think so, Clay. Too much has changed over the last few days."

After a pause in the conversation, Clay asked, "What happened when you two were kidnapped?"

Todd told his friend the story about the kidnapping and escape.

Clay listened intently at the fascinating story. He was amazed at how Todd had managed to get free and get away from their captors.

When Todd told about Denise's injury and rescue, Clay realized there were things about Todd he had never known before.

As Todd finished his story, Clay asked, "What about you and Denise?"

Todd responded, "What do you mean?"

Clay said, "Todd, you and Denise spent a lot of time together. How do you feel about her?"

Todd got up and walked to the warm heater and turned to Clay. He thought, "*Maybe this would be a good time to talk to Clay about my feelings toward Denise.*"

He told Clay, "I've never felt this way about anyone before in my whole life. Clay, when I thought I might lose her out there, I really became desperate. I prayed for the first time in my life. I swear, I prayed hard."

Clay asked, "Then you and Denise have become close. Right?"

Todd replied, "Right! Very close."

Clay asked, "Did anything happen between you two?"

Todd quickly responded, "No, Clay! Nothing...uh...nothing happened! We kissed a few times, but that's all!"

As the former teammates discussed the experiences of the past week, Todd began to feel better. He was glad to have a friend that would sit down with him and listen to his story.

Time seemed to pass quickly for Todd. It felt good to visit with Clay again. When Clay got up to leave, he asked Todd, "What time is Denise's operation?"

Todd responded, "7 a.m.! We'll have to leave early if we are going to visit with her before the surgery."

Clay said, "Dad is going fishing tomorrow; he always gets up early. I'll be here at 5:30 in the morning." He paused, "By the way, would you like to stay with me tonight?"

"Thanks Clay, but I would like to stay here tonight."

As Clay went to the door, he replied, "Okay, see ya at 5:30!"

Todd placed his hand out for Clay to shake and remarked, "Thanks for coming over, Clay. I needed to talk to someone."

Clay responded, "See ya in the morning."

Todd watched his friend leave before going into the kitchen. There wasn't much to choose from, but he put together a small snack.

His mind was full of thoughts—being alone, Denise's surgery, and Poppy coming home. He couldn't wait to take a bath and go to bed. Maybe tomorrow he could settle down and feel more like himself again.

· · · · · · · ● · · · · · · · · ·

When Denise finished telling her parents about the kidnapping, her mother got up, went to the bed, and took Denise's hand. The grateful mother said, "I'm so thankful it's over."

Mr. Poole added, "Amen!"

Mrs. Poole continued, "Denise, I didn't rest any while you were gone. I was so afraid they would do something to you, I...I prayed almost the entire time you were gone."

Mr. Poole stated, "I'm glad Todd was there to protect you!"

Denise wanted to assure her parents that Todd had taken good care of her. She told them, "Todd was a real gentleman the whole time we were out there. He treated me like I was somebody special. On top of everything else, he saved my life more than once."

Her mother asked, "Did you develop a close relationship?"

Denise answered, "I think so."

Her mother responded, "How does he feel about you?"

Denise shook her head, "I'm not sure, but I think he likes me."

They quickly turned their attention to the door as someone knocked several times. Denise and her mother said at the same time, "Come in!"

Mr. Poole helped open the door as Mandi and several classmates came in the door. They had several balloons and a vase of flowers. The balloons read, "GET WELL!"

Mandi was the first one to Denise's bedside. She said, "It sure is good to have you home!"

The other two girls agreed.

Denise smiled and told them, "You don't know how good it feels to be back!"

Mrs. Pool remarked as she took the balloons and flowers to place them by the window, "They sure brighten up the room!"

The girls could tell that Denise was weak and tired, so they stayed only a few minutes before leaving.

Not long after the girls left, there was another knock on the door. When Mr. Poole opened the door, Darren Hornsby asked if he could see Denise.

Darren went to Denise and hugged her. Mrs. Poole noticed that Denise appeared to become tense when Darren sat down. The former boyfriend asked how she was feeling, then he wanted to know about the surgery.

Denise told him about the operation and how the doctors were going to set her leg.

Darren asked if it would be okay if he could be with the family during the surgery.

Denise tightened up at Darren's statement.

Mrs. Poole decided she needed to answer that question, and said, "Darren, maybe you better let that be a family affair. We'll be glad to call you when the doctors are through, but I think it would be better if you didn't come tomorrow."

Denise was relieved at her mother's wisdom, and agreed with her.

Mr. Poole commented, "Someone will call you when it is over. You couldn't do anything if you were here, anyway!"

Darren agreed not to come and gave Mr. Poole his phone number.

When Darren left, Denise looked at her mother and said, "Thank you! You always seem to read my mind. I feel like Todd will be here, and that would create a tense situation."

After the sun had gone down, darkness filled the sky. The city began to glow with different colored lights. Mr. Poole told his wife, "We should leave and let Denise get some rest. They'll start early in the morning."

Bettie Poole raised her eyebrow and stated, "I just got Denise back, and I'm staying right here tonight!"

Denise smiled and told her mother, "It's okay, Mom! I'm in good hands. Go home and get some rest tonight."

Her mother looked at her daughter in the eyes and said, "I'm staying right here, and that's final!"

Denise looked at her surprised father and said, "Guess you're on your own tonight!"

Don Poole made a list of things to bring the next morning, kissed his wife and daughter good-bye and left.

Denise and her mother talked about Todd and the kidnapping incident until it was time to settle down for the night. Denise felt as though a tremendous load had been lifted from her shoulders. She was in a hospital instead of being in her own bed, but at least now she was safe.

•••••••••●•••••••••

Todd had never been in a hospital waiting room. He was fascinated by the different families waiting for doctors to report on loved ones. He watched as people drank coffee and soft drinks, read newspaper, and talked with other families. Several people had ministers with them. He wondered what they talked about at times like this.

Todd looked at Clay, who was sleeping in a large chair. He noticed Mr. Poole, who had just glanced at Clay. Todd remarked, "I don't think Clay is used to getting up this early."

Mr. Poole laughed and replied, "It looks as if he's sleeping pretty good."

The Pooles hadn't talked much since leaving Denise's room. They both had shown confidence in the doctors, but Todd felt they were concerned and worried about the surgery.

Time seemed to drag. Every time Todd looked at the clock on the wall, he wondered if it had stopped. He noticed that each time a doctor entered the waiting room, everyone would look up in nervous anticipation. Everyone, that is, except Clay, who was almost snoring.

Mr. Poole asked his wife and Todd if they wanted a snack, but both were anxious about Denise and declined the offer.

After what seemed an eternity, Denise's doctor called for them. They quickly followed him through a door into a conference room. As they were leaving, a red-eyed Clay stuttered, "Who...Wh...Where's everyone going?"

Todd answered, "We'll be right back!"

As they entered the conference room, the doctor reassured them, "Everything went as expected. We put two pins in her leg to hold the bone in place. She will be fine and should be able to go home in two or three days."

Mr. Poole asked, "What about the infection?"

The doctor replied, "That's why we want to keep her a couple of days. She's on antibiotics, and we don't expect any complications."

Mrs. Poole asked, "When will we be able to see her?"

The doctor looked at his watch and answered, "She will be in recovery another hour, then we will send her to her room. You can see her then."

Mr. Poole said, "Let's go eat! I'm buying lunch!"

Todd remarked, "We better not forget Clay."

Mr. Poole told Todd, "We'll get him as we go through the waiting room."

After eating in the hospital's cafeteria, they immediately went to Denise's room to see her.

Denise was asleep as Todd carefully opened the door.

He was the first one to her bed. She looked so innocent as he stood over her.

Mrs. Poole went to the opposite side of the bed and took her daughter's hand. Denise's eyes slowly opened and then closed. A faint smile appeared on her lips as she tried to speak. The words were slurred as she tried to recover her senses.

Clay stayed behind Todd and watched his friend look at Denise. He knew they had developed a strong friendship. He wondered how this would affect Todd's future.

After Denise seemed fully recovered, Todd and Clay decided to leave. Todd knew she was having some discomfort and felt it would be better if he left. The pain medication was making her act strange, and that bothered him.

On the way home, they stopped to check on Poppy. He told them he was coming home the next day. Todd couldn't remember seeing him this excited.

He knew he had to get home to clean up Poppy's room. He wanted to have everything ready for him when he returned.

• • • • • • • ● • • • • • • • • • •

Poppy arrived home the next day to a clean, warm house. He was weak, and he would have to move cautiously until he could regain his strength.

Mrs. Poole called later that evening to tell Todd about Denise getting released the next day. She told him her daughter wanted him to come to see her when she got home.

Todd called Mandi to tell her about Denise coming home. Mandi had asked him to notify her so she could make the first day home a memorable one.

• • • • • • • • • ● • • • • • • • • •

Denise was sitting in the backseat of the family car as it turned into the Poole's driveway. Tears filled her eyes when she saw yellow ribbons around the trees in their front yard.

Mandi and several of the cheerleaders were waiting for her.

Seeing friends made Denise feel good to finally be home.

Todd and Mr. Poole helped Denise get out of the car. Todd gave her a set of crutches and walked beside her in case she started to fall. She told Todd, "I still feel awkward trying to walk with these clumsy crutches."

Both men helped her into the house and across the den to a comfortable sofa, where she propped her injured leg on a fluffy cushion.

The girls chattered non-stop for several minutes before Mandi said, "We need to leave so Denise can get some rest!"

After the girls left, the room grew silent. Denise looked around the den, took a deep breath and commented, "It feels so good to be home. It seems like it's been ages since I was here."

When Denise began to show signs of growing tired, Todd knew he needed to leave. Mrs. Poole went to another room so the two teenagers could have a few moments to themselves.

Denise looked at Todd with a seriousness he hadn't seen before. She said to him, "Todd, I'll never be able to thank you. I wouldn't be home now if you hadn't been with me."

Todd thought a moment before commenting, "I think it's time for you to stop thanking me. I didn't do anything for thanks. I'm glad it's over; now I want us to enjoy being together." He wanted to tell her how much she meant to him, but the words wouldn't come out of his mouth. He did manage to say, "I'm glad you are home. I've missed you."

He kissed her lips softly, and she put her arms around his neck. They held each other for several minutes before Todd started to leave. He told her, "I'll see you tomorrow. Maybe you'll feel better by then." After another kiss, Todd slowly turned and left.

∙ ∙ ∙ ∙ ∙ ∙ ∙ ∙ ● ∙ ∙ ∙ ∙ ∙ ∙ ∙ ∙

Monday morning, Todd entered his first period government class feeling unusually strange. He was caught by surprise because he hadn't expected to feel this way. He knew everyone was thinking about him and the kidnapping.

Everyone spoke to him and told him they were glad he was back, and almost everyone asked about Denise. When Mr. Thompson, the government teacher, saw Todd, he asked how he and Denise were doing.

Mr. Thompson could tell Todd was uncomfortable talking about the incident, and when class finally started, the subject was never mentioned. That was a tremendous relief to Todd.

Todd had decided not to play basketball. When it came time for athletic period, he went to the field house instead of the gym. Coach Berry was glad to see him. He asked Todd to come into his office. The coach asked Todd, "Would you like to sit down?"

"Thanks, Coach!"

"Todd, I talked to the Texas Eastern coach this morning, and he is interested in you playing football for them. He likes your size and arm. He feels like you would fit in their offensive scheme."

Todd felt excitement as Coach Berry talked about his future. Todd asked, "When can I visit them?"

Coach replied, "They would like for you to come over for a weekend visit in January."

Todd got up and said, "Thanks, Coach! I appreciate all you've done for me."

Coach Berry got out of his chair and put his hand on Todd's shoulder and said, "Todd, I know you miss your parents, and I want to do anything I can to help you. I can't take their place, but I can help you when you have a need."

Todd smiled and told his coach, "Thanks, Coach! I'll be calling on you for advice and help. I feel like I can come to you with any problem I have."

As Todd left the office, the coach said, "Good to have you back, Todd."

· · · · · · · · · · ● · · · · · · · · · · ·

The week before Christmas vacation, Denise and Todd were eating lunch together. Todd mentioned, "You're getting around pretty good on those crutches."

"I've gotten plenty of practice!"

"How much longer do you have to stay on them?"

Denise replied, "The doctor said maybe I'll be off them by the middle of January."

"Then, what?"

"I'll be in a walking cast for a while."

When they finished eating, Denise said, "Todd, I've talked to Mother and Dad, and we would like for you and Poppy to spend Christmas Day with us."

He was silent for a while, then said, "That would be great! The last two years, Poppy and I were alone. We'll both look forward to that!"

Todd took their lunch trash and threw it away while Denise got on her crutches.

When they started to class, Todd told her, "I've signed up for a driver's education course after Christmas. Clay told me this morning he would teach me how to drive. I should be able to get my driver's license pretty soon."

Denise was pleased and said, "Great! That'll be great."

They stopped outside of the school building, where they were alone. Todd then told her in confidence about his trust fund and how much his parents had tried to take care of him before their untimely deaths. He didn't want everyone to know about the money. He said, "When I get that money, I'll be able to get a car and be like everyone else."

Denise knew he was self-conscious about not being able to drive and never mentioned it to him. She knew his confidence had grown since the kidnapping. His future was looking brighter each day. He would probably get a football scholarship, have his own money, and be able to drive his own car. All of this was helping Todd to develop a more outgoing personality, and she liked that.

• • • • • • • • • ● • • • • • • • • •

Denise picked Todd and Poppy up around midmorning on Christmas Day and took them to the Poole's house. It was a cold but sunny day, and Todd was looking forward to being with a family for this special time of the year.

When they arrived, there were several cars in the front of the house. Denise had told Todd that there would be aunts, uncles, cousins, and grandparents eating with them. He was excited, but was also apprehensive about meeting the family Denise had told him about.

Todd and Poppy were introduced to the family when they entered the house. Poppy immediately took up with Denise's grandparents and seemed to feel at home with them.

The meal was much more than Todd could ever remember seeing on a single table. He found himself enjoying the meal and visiting with the family.

Around mid-afternoon, gifts were exchanged. Todd had taken what little money he had, borrowed some from Poppy, and bought Denise a dainty necklace with a football and his number, 10, engraved on it. As she opened the small package and saw it, she smiled and said, "Ooh, Todd! It's precious!"

She leaned over, hugged him and whispered in his ear, "I love it."

He was slightly embarrassed receiving this sign of affection in front of everyone, but he had a wonderful feeling inside. It had been a long time since he had given someone a gift, and he liked that sensation.

When Todd opened his gift, he found a beautiful watch. It was nicer than anything he had received since his parent's death. He smiled and said, "Thank you. It's great!" Denise made it easy for him to hug her. This was his best Christmas in years.

When Denise took Todd and Poppy home, Poppy thanked her and started to the house. He knew the young couple wanted to be alone. Denise and Todd stayed in the car. They finally had some time to themselves.

Todd told her how much the day had meant to him and Poppy. When he kissed Denise good night, her warm soft lips sent a chill up his back. This had been a special day, and Denise was a very special person. Being with such a lovely person was hard for Todd to comprehend. He had been alone for so many years; he wanted to remember this moment forever.

When they finished kissing, they held each other tightly. Denise whispered, "Todd, I think I love you."

His heart must have skipped a beat, because he had never felt such an overpowering feeling of emotion in his life. As he held her even tighter, he muttered, "I...I think I love you, too."

CHAPTER 10

The last weekend in January was a big one for Todd and Clay. They visited Texas Eastern State University on a recruiting trip. It wasn't a large school, but Todd didn't particularly want to go to a big school where he would just be a number. He was looking forward to entering a small college and playing football. .

The two prospects were greeted by Coach Preston when they arrived on campus. He introduced them to several of the football players. One of them, named Dan, asked if they would like to go to a basketball game on campus that night. This would give them the opportunity to meet some of the students; they quickly accepted the invitation.

Arriving at the game, Dan introduced Todd and Clay to two college girls, Carol and Penny. Both young women were nice looking and friendly. Todd and Clay grinned at each other as they entered the playing arena with the two attractive coeds at their side.

Sitting with Carol and Penny during the game, Todd began feeling uncomfortable. Denise was the only girl he was dating, and he began to feel guilty. He and Denise weren't committed to each other officially, but they enjoyed being together. Todd noticed Clay wasn't much more at ease than he was.

After the game, Dan and the girls escorted the two football prospects to a reception at a nearby club. There was drinking taking place, and Todd drank a small amount; however, he didn't care for this new taste he was experiencing. Being with college students was a bit intimidating to Todd. He didn't like peer pressure telling him what to do, but he drank to be like the other students.

Clay also drank a small amount. He did not care for the strong drink, either.

Everyone was friendly and tried to encourage them to sign with Texas Eastern; however, they were expecting to get that kind of reception. Coach Berry had talked to both athletes before they left so they would know what to expect on this trip.

Todd finally got Clay aside and asked, "Did you drink much?"

"Naw! Just a little bit! It's kinda strong, isn't it?"

"It sure is! It burned me all the way down. I hope Denise doesn't find out I drank that stuff!"

Clay raised his eyebrows and said, "Speaking of Denise, what would she think if she knew about Carol and Penny?"

Todd quickly responded, "Don't you ever mention that to her. I feel guilty enough without her finding out about this evening!"

Clay laughed, "Don't worry! I don't want Cindy to know about this, either!"

Todd looked around to see if anyone was watching and said, "The last thing Denise told me before I left was not to mess around with any of these college women! Now look what's happened. How did we manage to pick up these girls?"

Clay shook his head and exclaimed, "Dan introduced us, and the next thing I knew...they were...uh...hanging all over us!"

Both athletes looked around when Carol said, "Come on Todd, let's dance."

Todd looked back at Clay as she took his hand and led him to the dance floor.

Clay snickered as he heard Todd mumble, "Oh, man!" Before he knew what was happening, he too was dancing.

Around midnight, Todd and Clay told the girls they had to leave. Carol and Penny unexpectedly escorted them to the dorm. Carol took Todd's arm and Penny took Clay's hand as they left the party.

They drove around the campus several times, as the girls pointed out certain buildings and places of interest. Finally, they arrived at the dormitory where Todd and Clay were to spend the night. Both girls huddled close to the two football prospects.

Todd could feel sweat forming around his neck. All he could think about was Denise walking up to the car and getting mad at him.

After kissing the girls several times, Todd and Clay said good night to Carol and Penny and got out of the car.

When they finally entered their room, Todd leaned against the closed door and exclaimed, "Wow, have you ever had a first date like that?"

Clay remarked, "I didn't think they were ever going to let us out of the car!"

"We weren't rude to 'em, were we?"

"Naw, I don't think so!"

"I hope Denise and Cindy don't find out about tonight!" Todd mentioned.

Clay responded, "You think all college girls are like those two?"

"I doubt it! If I hadn't been dating Denise,…well…that could have been a real adventure!"

"I'll say!" Clay exclaimed, then continued, "Todd, remember Coach Berry told us they would show us a good time!"

"Yeah! Right! I don't think he was talking about Carol and Penny!"

"Probably not!" Clay said, then continued, "I've drunk beer before, but that stuff we had tonight was stout!"

Todd said, "I didn't see many football players there; wonder where they were."

Clay answered, "I don't know, but let's get to bed! We have to get up early to meet with the coaches tomorrow morning."

Todd, who had gone to the restroom, asked Clay, "Wonder how you get this taste out of your mouth."

Clay laughed and commented, "Brush your teeth and get in bed. You'll forget about it by morning."

Neither of them slept well that night because of the excessive noise in the dorm. At breakfast the next morning, Coach Preston ate with the recruits. Todd asked him, "Are all dorms as loud as the one we stayed in last night?"

The coach smiled, and answered, "No! It was just Friday night. During the week, we are very strict on noise levels. We require our athletes to spend a certain amount of time each night in study. Our players are here for an education, and we stay on them pretty hard."

Todd and Clay were shown the campus and other facilities. They were much more impressed by the school on Saturday than they had been the night before with Carol and Penny.

The coaching staff left good impressions on both young men. They were friendly and seemed to be truly interested in their athletes. Todd and Clay knew college football would be different from high school, but they were looking forward to a new chapter in their lives.

They started home Saturday afternoon. During the trip, Clay asked, "Where is Denise going to school?"

Todd replied, "She's thinking about SMU in Dallas!"

Clay said, "At least that's close!"

"Yeah, but if she ever finds out about those girls last night...well you know...she might as well go to Kalamazoo!" Todd continued, "What about Cindy?"

Clay responded, "If I go to Texas Eastern, she will probably go there, also."

A week later, Todd and Clay were both offered football scholarships to Texas Eastern, and both signed letters of intent in February.

The local newspaper was present to take pictures of Clay, his parents, and Coach Berry as he signed his letter of intent.

Poppy and Coach Berry stood with Todd as pictures were taken of him signing his papers.

·············●·············

Several weeks later, Todd reminded Clay, "Now remember, I have never driven a car before."

Clay said sarcastically, "Sure, you haven't!"

As Todd and Clay walked to the car, Todd stated, "Seriously Clay, I've never driven!"

Clay half-heartedly responded, "Okay! I believe you!"

Todd got in the driver's side and scooted into the seat and grabbed the steering wheel with both hands. A strange look came over his face, and he swallowed hard.

Clay stared at Todd a moment and asked, "You've...uh...really never driven a car before, have you?"

Todd replied, "That's what I've been trying to tell you!"

Clay muttered, "Man, I thought you were kidding!"

Todd asked, "What do I do first?"

"It would help to turn on the ignition and start the car."

"Okay!"

Todd reached for the key and started the car, immediately putting both hands firmly on the steering wheel. Then he asked, "Now what?"

Clay said, "Uh...I think we'd better buckle our seatbelts!"

After both had fastened their belts, Clay looked behind them, then said, "First, you need to put it in reverse and back out...reverse is "R" on the panel!"

Todd snapped, "I know that!"

Taking his right hand off the wheel, he roughly got the transmission in reverse, gunned the car, and held on as the car jumped into the street. Todd stomped the brakes, and they stopped as quickly as they started. The two friends looked at each other for a moment; Clay repeated, "First time, right?"

Todd replied, "Yep!"

Clay said, "Okay, *ease* the car into drive...the "D"...but, I guess you knew that!"

Todd worked the gear into "D" and slowly started down the street, being very careful not to give the car too much gas this time. With both hands firmly on the steering wheel, Todd stared straight ahead.

Clay told him, "Relax, you're doing fine!"

As they slowly gained speed, Clay mentioned, "There's a stop sign up—"

But, before he could finish the sentence, the tires squealed when Todd stomped the breaks. When Todd stopped approximately thirty yards from the stop sign, Clay mentioned, "Uh...Todd, you really need to get a little closer to that stop sign before you stop!"

"I didn't know your brakes were so sensitive!"

"Any brakes are sensitive if you stomp them!"

They eased up to the stop sign and stopped. Clay told him, "Push the blinker up and turn right."

After about thirty minutes of driving, Todd began to relax and seemed to be driving very well. After his first driving lesson, he drove the car to his house, stopped properly, and the two guys got out.

Todd handed Clay the keys and thanked him for helping him take his first lesson, then asked, "Would you like to come in for a cold drink?"

"Thanks, but I need to get home. I have a date with Cindy tonight."

Within two weeks of his eighteenth birthday, Todd had completed his driver's education class, received his driver's license, and was feeling rather comfortable driving Clay's car. He now looked forward to having his own "set of wheels."

When Todd and Denise left school on Friday afternoon, they planned to have a date and go to a movie in Dallas. On the way to Todd's house, she asked him, "Now that you have your license, would you like to drive my car tonight?"

He responded, "Sure, I'd love to!"

When he got home, he became jittery thinking about driving in a city. He showered, fixed his hair, and brushed his teeth. Then he waited patiently for Denise to pick him up.

On the trip to Dallas, Todd was nervous but had no trouble driving them to the theater. Driving was a new adventure, but he became more secure each time.

On the way home, he told Denise, "I can't wait to get my own car! Then, I won't have to depend on others to do things for me."

While he drove home, Denise could see the excitement in his eyes. She watched him and thought about how nice looking he was. He was also a gentleman. He always put her interest first in everything they did. She knew his parents would be proud of him if they could see him now.

•••••••••●••••••••

Several days before Todd's birthday, Denise told Clay, "We want to make sure he is surprised."

Clay replied, "Okay, I'll get him to go somewhere with me. However, that won't be easy because he is going to want to be with you on his birthday."

Denise said, "That's true. I'll just have to have an excuse not to be with him that night. I'll think of something."

Clay and Denise worked on an idea for a surprise birthday party for Todd. After considerable planning, Denise made sure it would be a memorable one for him.

Clay stopped Todd between classes on Tuesday and said, "Hey bud, you've got the big eighteen coming up Friday!"

Todd responded, "That's right, number eighteen!"

Clay asked, "You got any plans?"

"Not yet!"

"Why don't we go to Dallas and celebrate."

"You mean double date?"

Clay hesitated before saying, "I thought you might like to do something different to celebrate *the* birthday."

Todd continued, "I want to check with Denise first. We may do something Friday night."

Clay paused, then said, "Okay, ask Denise; but if you two don't do anything, just the two of us will celebrate."

Todd replied, "I'll let you know something later."

When Todd ate lunch with Denise, he asked her, "Would you like to go to a movie Friday night and help celebrate my eighteenth birthday?"

Denise paused and said, "I'm sorry Todd, but...uh...my parents are taking me to my grandparents this weekend, and we're...uh... leaving after school Friday." She could see the hurt in his eyes and felt guilty about hurting his feelings.

Her answer was a complete surprise to him. He stuttered, "Oh… uh… okay."

She said, "I'm sorry, I know you want to do something special on your birthday, but I don't have much of a choice."

She thought, "*There I go lying again.*"

Todd said, "That's okay. Clay has asked me to do something with him. We'll have a good time." He didn't know why he said that because he knew he didn't really mean it. He wanted to be with Denise, not Clay.

Denise watched him when he left. He almost reminded her of a whipped puppy. She knew he would be surprised about the party and would forgive her.

Denise's parents helped her rent a place at the lake that promised to be ideal for a party. She could hardly wait to see his surprised face when he realized he had been tricked.

When Clay picked Todd up on Friday evening, he said, "Perk-up, bud! You're eighteen today. Feel any different?"

Todd replied, "Nope!"

Clay was supposed to have Todd at the lake house at 7 p.m. He had about thirty minutes he was going to have to kill. He asked Todd, "Mind if we go by the lake on the way to Dallas?"

A depressed Todd responded, "Sounds okay to me."

Clay could tell his friend was not happy. He knew Todd wanted to be with Denise, and in a few minutes his buddy would be in a lot better spirits.

Todd couldn't imagine why they were driving down the back roads at the lake. It was almost dark, and the water was becoming smooth. He noticed the lights from across the lake. They were reflecting off the calm water, creating a beautiful picture in a variety of colors.

When they passed a small park, he thought, "*This would be a good place to bring Denise sometime.*" He hadn't seen her in several hours, and he was already missing her. He could tell it was going to be a long, lonesome weekend.

As they came to the lakehouse, Clay commented, "Hey, a good friend of my family lives here; do you mind if I stop a minute?"

Todd replied, "No. Why should I?"

Clay stopped the car, and said, "Come with me. These are great people. Let me introduce you to'em."

Todd responded, "That's all right. I'll just wait in the car."

Clay said, more firmly, "Get out! You're going to like them!"

Not expecting a surprise, Todd reluctantly got out of the car and walked to the front door with Clay. Clay knocked on the door. It slowly opened into a dark room. Suddenly, the lights came on and a room full of classmates shouted, "*Surprise*!"

Todd couldn't believe what he was seeing. He quickly jumped backwards, looked at Clay and said, "You *rat*! You set me up!"

Denise put her arms around Todd's neck, kissed him, and said, "Happy Birthday!"

Todd was embarrassed that his friends had surprised him so completely.

Clay noticed that his friend, who had a big smile on his face, had gone from depressed to excited.

Mr. and Mrs. Poole came to Todd. Don Poole shook his hand and wished him a happy birthday, while Bettie Poole hugged him and whispered in his ear, "Happy birthday, Todd. You're a very special person." Todd felt a chill run up his spine. What had started out as just a dull Friday night without Denise had turned into a surprise eighteenth birthday party.

Several of his teammates—Stanley Wilson, Bill Blackwell, and Pat Deen, along with others—wished him a happy birthday. He hadn't stopped to realize that he was in the spotlight. He was having a great time, and his attitude about this evening had changed tremendously. Being with Denise and friends had made for a jubilant Friday evening.

After the Pooles and other parents went to the back room, the teenagers danced and visited. Following several dances, Denise and Todd sneaked out back to be alone for a few minutes.

The calm water reflected various lights from the distant shore and a moon that was just coming up. It made a very romantic setting. Denise said, "Todd, I'm sorry I lied to you about being gone this weekend, but I really wanted to surprise you."

Todd smiled and commented, "I love it! I think it was a great idea. I can't believe you and Clay fooled me so. However, I now owe both of you."

Denise knew he would probably try to get even with them sometime in the future for surprising him. As they stood there in the moonlight, they put their arms around each other and kissed.

•••••••••●•••••••••

When Todd entered the field house for athletics on Monday, Coach Berry called him aside. He said to him, "Todd, I've been thinking about the commitment you made after Denise's injury. Have you thought anymore about it?"

Todd replied, "Yes sir, I have. You've seen me at church with Denise. However, I am still confused about where God is leading me."

"Have you talked to anyone about it?"

"No sir. I've thought about talking to the preacher, but never have gotten around to it."

Coach Berry said, "Brother Bill would be a good person to talk to when you get ready. I was wondering if it was bothering you as badly as it did when you two got home."

Todd responded, "Not as bad, but I still wonder if I'm going in the right direction."

Coach said, "I'll be praying for you."

Todd acknowledged, "Thanks, Coach, I appreciate that."

After athletics, Todd, Poppy and Coach Berry went to Don Poole's law office to accept the check from the trust fund. Mr. Poole had been in contact with Mr. Goldsmith, the trustee in charge of Todd's fund. Mr. Goldsmith was present when Todd got to the office. Mr. Poole introduced everyone and invited them to have a seat.

Mr. Goldsmith said, "Todd, you were just a little fellow the last time I saw you. You sure turned into a nice-looking young man."

Todd's heart was pounding when he answered, "Th...hank you, sir. Do you remember my grandfather, Poppy?"

Mr. Goldsmith replied, "Sure, but it's been a long time." He continued, "Todd, I'm so glad your parents had the foresight to take care of you with this fund. I highly recommend you talk to someone about investing this money wisely."

Todd answered, "Yes sir, I will."

After signing the necessary papers, Mr. Goldsmith handed him a check for $350,000. Todd was so weak in the knees, he didn't know how to act.

After Mr. Goldsmith left, Todd, Poppy and Coach Berry visited in Mr. Poole's office. Todd asked, "What do I do next?"

Mr. Poole answered, "The first thing you need to do is deposit that check in the bank."

When the check had been deposited, Poppy and Todd went to a local car dealer. Poppy helped Todd buy a new car he had been looking at for several weeks, a bright red Mustang.

Once they had taken care of insurance matters, Todd drove his grandfather home. Then he headed for Denise's house. He could hardly wait for her to see his new car. She was expecting him and came out the front door as soon as he stopped.

He experienced several new feelings. He was eighteen, dated one of the prettiest girls in school, and now had his own car. He couldn't describe how he felt.

Denise got in and exclaimed, "It's beautiful! Is it yours?"

"All mine! Want to go for a ride?"

"Sure!"

Todd said, "Let's find Clay. I want him to see it!"

After driving around, feeling like a real teenager, they found Clay leaving the field house. Clay looked up, saw Todd, and shouted, "Hey! That yours?"

"Yep! Hop in!"

While Todd drove Denise and Clay around town, Clay teased Todd. He joked, "Todd, you gonna stop before or after you get to that stop sign."

Todd remarked, "These brakes aren't as sensitive as the ones on your car."

They all enjoyed riding in Todd's new car. When Clay got out, he shook Todd's hand and said, "It's a beaut, and you deserve it!"

Todd replied, "Thanks, see ya tomorrow."

When he drove Denise home, Mr. Poole had just gotten out of his car. He walked over to Todd and said, "That's a good looking car. Why don't we go out to eat and celebrate?"

Bettie and Don Poole followed Todd and Denise to a restaurant for supper and celebrated this new chapter in Todd's life.

When he got home that night, he lay in his bed but couldn't go to sleep. He was too excited to relax. He thought about his new car, driving Denise around town, and about how good he felt.

He turned on a lamp, picked up a western novel and started to read. As he read about a cattle drive in Texas, he finally dozed into a light sleep.

CHAPTER 11

On a Friday afternoon in early April, the Poole's doorbell rang. Denise, thinking it was Todd, opened the door excitedly. She was totally surprised to see Darren Hornsby standing there. She swallowed hard and said, "Uh...hello ...Darren."

She could tell he was uneasy as he asked in a somber voice, "Mind if I come in?"

"Uh...no...come on in." Her heart beat rapidly from the surprise of seeing him.

He said, "Denise, the only way I know how to handle this is to get straight to the point. I'm sorry for the way I treated you last fall. You didn't deserve that."

Denise responded, "Darren, that was a long time ago. I've almost forgotten that it ever happened."

He replied, "Well, I haven't. I think about that stupid mistake all the time."

"Darren, forget about it; it's long passed."

"Could you ever forgive me?"

"I forgot about that a long time ago. Sure, I'll forgive you."

Todd was totally surprised when he came around the corner and saw Darren Hornsby's car at Denise's house. He thought, "She hasn't seen Darren in months. What's he doing here?"

His temper flared as he stomped the accelerator. His tires squealed as his new car sped off. The only thing he could think about was Denise and Darren being together. He had never been jealous before, and he didn't know how to handle that terrible feeling.

Inside the house, Denise heard Todd's tires scream as he raced off. She didn't see him, but she knew who it was. She could hardly listen to Darren's conversation for thinking about Todd being mad at her.

Denise and Todd had never had a disagreement. Their relationship had been unusually smooth. They both respected and admired each other. Now Todd had seen Darren's car at her house and sped off in a fury.

Darren asked, "Is there any hope of you ever dating me again?"

Denise didn't hesitate when she answered, "Darren, I forgot about the incident a long time ago, but I am dating a person I like and respect very much. I would never hurt him in any way. You and I will probably always be friends, but I don't see us dating again."

Darren stayed and visited for several more minutes before he left.

Immediately after his departure, Denise ran to the phone and called Todd's house. Poppy answered the phone. After she asked for Todd, the old man told her, "Todd left to go to your house several minutes ago. I haven't seen him since he left."

She then called Clay's house, but he had gone on a date with Cindy. He wouldn't be home until later.

Denise got in her car and drove around town looking for Todd, but no one seemed to know where he was. She remembered he often went to the football field when he was upset or wanted to be alone. When she arrived at the stadium, he wasn't there. Now she became concerned.

Todd drove to a near-by town and saw three ex-students he knew. The former students had purchased several packs of beer and asked Todd if he wanted to join them.

Todd had never been mad at Denise before, but the thought of Darren's car in her driveway irritated him. He immediately accepted the invitation. He parked his car in a vacant lot and got in the car with the former students. The four of them drove around town and drank beer. Todd still didn't like the taste, but tonight he didn't care because he was trying to get over the hurt of seeing Denise and Darren together.

He wasn't a drinker, and it didn't take very much beer for him to get light-headed. It wasn't too long before he was drunk.

Realizing Todd was getting drunk, one of the guys asked Todd if he needed help getting home.

Todd, trying to maintain his dignity, refused any help. He told them, "I'm ...just...fine. I've...got...my own...car. I'll get...myself...home."

Another guy asked, "Are you sure you're okay?"

Todd staggered to his car, and finally answered, "Sure, I'll get...myself...home." He slowly got in his car and struggled to get his seat belt fastened. After the buckle snapped into place, Todd started his car and spun the tires as he drove off.

One of the drinkers said, "I sure hope he makes it home without anything happening to him."

Another one agreed, "Yeah, me too."

As Todd started home, he began to feel sick. His stomach was turning over and over; he felt as though he would vomit. He turned off onto a small road, got out and threw-up. He thought his insides were coming out. He had never been this sick in his life. He got on his hands and knees and wondered if he would ever stop.

He had enough sense to know he didn't want to mess up his new car. He wouldn't get back in it until he was through, which could be several minutes. He had thrown-up on his clothes, and he knew he would probably get some in his car.

Todd wiped his hands on some grass and got as much off his clothes as possible. He staggered back to his car and slowly got in it. Again, he struggled to get the seatbelt fastened. He was about to give up when it finally snapped.

He hated the fact that he didn't have command of his mind and body. He was the type that always wanted to be in control, much like he did when he and Denise had been kidnapped.

He struggled, but finally got his car turned around and drove back onto the main road.

Todd was having difficulty controlling his speed and judging the curves. Before he could slow himself down, he missed a sharp curve. He was suddenly out of control, and the car flipped over and over.

Was he dreaming, or was this really happening? Everything seemed to be in slow motion. The world was spinning around him. Glass was breaking and flying around in the car. His head snapped back against the headrest. Finally, the car came to a stop, upside down and in a ditch.

Nothing made sense anymore. He couldn't move. What was wrong? Would the car catch on fire?

The seatbelt held him in his seat, and he felt trapped. Why couldn't he get out? Why wouldn't his hands work? In fact, he couldn't move anything. This had to be a bad dream.

Everything began to become faint as he visualized Denise's face. She was so pretty. Then everything went blank.

A car behind Todd saw the accident. The driver picked up his cell phone and called 911 for help. He got out and ran over to the car and tried to talk to Todd. By this time, several other cars had stopped.

Pat Deen, one of Todd's teammates, got out of a car and ran to the accident. He exclaimed, "That looks like Todd Perry's new car!" When he saw Todd upside down and motionless, he said, "Oh no, it is Todd!"

The first man at the scene told everyone, "An ambulance is on the way. We won't move him unless a fire starts. Everyone keep your eyes open for any sign of fire!"

The ambulance arrived shortly, and the paramedics immediately started to prepare Todd for removal from the vehicle. Since he was unconscious, they took all precautions. They quickly immobilized his neck.

A fire truck and crew arrived to make sure there wasn't a fire, and several of that crew helped remove Todd from the car. They were very cautious as they moved him. They knew any wrong move could cause irreparable damage.

He was carefully placed on a backboard, put in the ambulance, and rushed to the local hospital.

A doctor and several nurses were waiting when the young victim was brought to the emergency room. The nurses quickly checked all vital signs. When the doctor checked for reflexes, he became concerned when Todd's extremities showed little or no response. After several tests, the doctor ordered Todd to be air lifted to a Dallas facility.

Clay and Cindy were at the local hangout when Pat rushed in and told them about Todd's accident. Clay asked, "What about Denise; was she with him?"

Pat answered, "No! He was by himself!"

Clay turned to Cindy, "Let's find Denise!"

They hurried to the Poole's house. When Denise opened the door, she could tell by Clay's expression something serious had happened. She quickly asked, "What's wrong? Has something happened to Todd?"

Clay answered, "Todd was in a serious accident. He flipped his car!"

Denise covered her mouth with both hands and asked, "How serious is it?"

"We don't know! He's at the hospital now. You want to go with us?"

Denise ran to her parents and told them about the accident, then quickly got into the car with Cindy and Clay. As Clay sped off, Denise uttered, "I knew something bad was going to happen! I just knew it!" Her heart was racing as anxiety and concern for Todd built in her mind.

Clay asked, "Why weren't you with him tonight? It's not like Todd to go some place without you."

Denise replied, "That's the problem! When Todd came by tonight, Darren was at my house. I heard tires squeal and knew it was Todd. I figured he got mad and spun off. Why did Darren have to come over? Why?"

Cindy commented, "Stop blaming yourself; it's not your fault."

Denise replied, "I just hope it's not serious."

Clay drove up to the emergency entrance and parked his car. The three teenagers quickly got out and ran into the hospital.

Denise asked, "Where's Todd Perry?"

When the local doctor recognized Denise, he took her, Cindy, and Clay aside and told them, "We don't know how seriously he is hurt, yet. There does appear to be some paralysis in his arms and legs. What I mean is his reflexes aren't what I would like for him to have. Since he's unconscious, we don't know the extent of his injuries."

Denise put her hands over her mouth and fought back the tears that filled her eyes. Clay put his arm around her and pulled her closer to him.

The doctor continued, "I've called for a careflight helicopter to airlift him to Dallas. We want him to get the best care possible."

Denise's parents came through the emergency door and saw her crying and rushed to her. She leaned her head against her father and cried, "Dad, Todd may be paralyzed! They're sending him to Dallas by helicopter so he can get better care."

Denise asked the doctor if she could see Todd. He took her to the room where Todd was lying. Tears were running down her cheeks as she took Todd's hand and held it. She quietly asked, "Why Todd? Why did you have to do this?"

Cindy and Clay stood close to the door and watched Denise talk to the motionless figure. Tears filled Clay's eyes as he thought about playing football with Todd.

He remembered how nervous Todd was when he learned to drive. Todd was smart and became a good driver in a short period of time.

He also thought about the recruiting trip they had taken to Texas Eastern. The idea of something serious happening to his best friend was hard to swallow. As Clay reminisced, Cindy huddled a little closer and put both arms around him.

Denise held Todd's limp hand until they started to get him ready for transport. She couldn't believe how many tubes and wires had been attached to his body. However, she knew that each one was important.

Clay stepped away while the doctor prepared Todd for the flight to Dallas.

He asked a police officer standing at the door, "What happened to cause Todd's accident?"

The officer told Clay, "We think he had been drinking and lost control of his car."

Clay responded, "Todd doesn't drink!"

"We're pretty sure he had been drinking tonight. Was he upset about something?"

Denise heard the conversation and responded, "Yes sir. He was upset at me."

She told the officer what had happened earlier in the day. As they talked about the incident, they heard the pounding of helicopter blades when it approached the hospital. Dirt whirled around as the big careflight helicopter finally rested on the landing pad.

Don and Bettie Poole told Denise, "We're going to get Poppy. He needs to know what's happened. We'll take him to Dallas if he wants to go."

Clay said, "I'm calling my parents. I plan to go to Dallas as soon as possible. Denise, do you want to go with me?"

Denise responded, "Sure! I'm ready!"

Don Poole warned, "Clay, be careful. We don't need anything else tragic to happen tonight."

Clay replied, "Yes sir! Don't worry, I'll be careful."

Cindy exclaimed, "I'm going, too! Give me time to call my parents!"

They all stood and watched as Todd was loaded into the helicopter.

Denise asked if she could go with Todd, but that wasn't permissible, so she reluctantly stepped aside.

When Todd was set in the aircraft, Denise thought about their rescue in a helicopter after being kidnapped in the fall. It didn't seem that long ago that she was the one being strapped into a helicopter. What a strange twist life had taken. She could now understand Todd's concern for her when he watched her as she was prepared for take-off.

Denise reasoned, "At least I wasn't in a life or death situation. Todd's life may be in jeopardy. What will I do if he dies? Die?" That was the first time she had thought about the possibility of his dying. What will I—?"

Her thoughts were broken as the big engines revved up, and dirt began to hit her in the face.

She prayed, "Please Lord! Let Todd be okay. Please!"

There was very little conversation as Clay raced to the Dallas hospital. Each one had special memories of Todd that went through their minds.

Denise thought about their time together in the wilderness and how Todd had masterminded their rescue. Now all she could do was pray that God would take care of him.

When the three teenagers got to the hospital, they found that Todd had regained consciousness. The doctor in the emergency room let Denise see him, but Clay and Cindy had to wait outside his room. She eased closer to his bed. Todd's eyes were the only thing that moved. He was confused and couldn't figure out what had happened to him.

Denise whispered, "Todd."

He asked, "What happened?"

"You were in an accident."

"Did I mess up my car?"

"I don't know; I haven't seen it."

"Where...am...I?"

"You're in a Dallas hospital."

"I can't...feel anything. What's...wrong?"

"I don't know, the doctors are checking."

Denise fought back tears; she knew she had to be strong talking to him.

A nurse came into the room and said, "We're taking him for some tests. If you would, wait in the waiting room. We'll get you when we're through."

"What kind of tests will he have?"

"We're going to run a CT scan."

"What's a CT scan?"

"It will give us a 3-D image of the spinal cord. It shows a better view of the soft tissue."

Denise moved to the waiting room with Clay and Cindy. While they sat there watching all of the activity involved in a major Dallas hospital, Clay remarked, "This is going to be a long, long night."

Mr. and Mrs. Poole came in with Poppy, who looked tired. He immediately asked, "How is he?"

Denise answered, "He talked some, but he's very confused. He doesn't know what happened."

Poppy said, "It's not like Todd to be careless."

Denise didn't say anything about Todd drinking. However, she felt guilty for not finding Todd after he left her house. If she could have explained there's nothing between her and Darren, Todd might not have been injured.

Clay paced back and forth, while Denise and Cindy sat in the uncomfortable chairs. Time seemed to stand still.

Finally, one of the doctors came to them. Talking to Denise, Poppy, and the Poole family, he said, "So far, everything has turned up negative. The best we can tell, there are no fractures. As to why he is showing signs of paralysis, we can't say. It could be from the trauma of the accident. Hopefully, he will start getting his reflexes back soon. The next few hours are going to be critical."

Denise asked, "What did the CT scan show?"

The doctor replied, "We have found no nerve damage in any of our tests. We will run an MRI first thing tomorrow morning."

Don Poole asked, "What will that show?"

"It gives us high resolution images of the damaged area. A neurologist will review all of our tests. At that point, we should have a fairly good idea of Todd's problem."

As he was talking, Coach Berry and his wife Beth came into the emergency room. They didn't say a word as the doctor continued, "Someone will be with him at all times until we know more. We'll let two at a time visit him. Try to stay positive when you're with him. Are there any questions?"

After answering all of the questions, Denise and Poppy went to see him first. Clay and Cindy explained to the Berrys what had happened and what tests had been run on Todd. Coach Berry was familiar with most of the tests, since some of his athletes had had some in the past.

Todd seemed to be a little more rational this time when Denise entered the room. Poppy asked, "How are you feeling, son?"

Todd explained, "I don't know. I have a funny tingling in my arms and legs. Other than that, I can't feel much."

He looked at Denise and continued, "Looks like I messed up this time."

Denise said, "Todd, I'm sorry. Why didn't you stop instead of running off? There's nothing between Darren and me, except we're just friends. That's all!"

Todd replied, "I don't know. I just wasn't thinking clearly I guess."

She bent over and kissed him on the cheek, and said, "Todd you're the only one I care about." Tears filled her eyes as she continued, "You're so important to me!"

A tear ran down the side of his face. He commented, "I can't even wipe away a tear. I've really messed up this time."

Poppy told him in a rough voice, "Son, the doctors haven't found anything wrong. I think you're going to be just fine."

Poppy left the two young people, and in a few minutes Coach Berry entered the room. They looked at each other before anything was said. Finally, Todd asked, "Coach, is God trying to get my attention?"

Coach Berry replied, "Looks to me like he has your attention."

Todd replied, "Coach, I messed up tonight. I saw some of our former students and drank some beer with them. I...guess I...uh...got drunk. I...I really let everyone down tonight. Everything is so fuzzy. I just can't remember very much."

Coach Berry responded, "I hate what's happened to you, but I am so glad you realized your mistake. Just make sure that something like this doesn't happen again."

Todd answered, "Don't worry. It won't. Coach, what if I am paralyzed? What then?"

Coach Berry reacted, "We're going to be positive about this whole incident. We're going to believe and pray that you're going to be okay."

Todd replied, "Thanks, Coach."

Coach Berry left, but Denise stayed with Todd.

Reality began to set in with Todd. For the first time, he had thoughts about a life of paralysis. That meant no more football, sports, or any of the things he loved to do.

Being dependent on someone else to take care of all his needs was unsettling.

As Denise held his hand, which he couldn't feel, he became depressed. He glanced at her out of the corner of his eyes and wondered, "*How will this affect my relationship with her? I can't ask her to live a life of taking care of me.*"

A tear rolled down his cheek when he said, "Denise, if I have to be paralyzed, I don't want to live. Maybe God will go ahead and take me now."

Denise snapped, "Stop it! I won't listen to you talk like that! You're going to be okay. I just know it!"

He answered, "We have to be realistic."

They were silent for several moments. Denise knew she had to keep him positive. She finally asked, "Todd, where's that strong person who was so determined to get free and take care of me when we were kidnapped?"

They very seldom, if ever, talked about the kidnapping, but she was determined not to let him quit. It was way too early to give up.

She continued, "Todd we don't have all the results back from your tests yet, and the ones we do have show no spinal injuries. We will not discuss paralysis; understand?"

He looked into her dark brown eyes and knew he couldn't argue with this attractive girl. For the first time since the accident, a faint smile came on his face as he muttered, "Okay, I understand."

Around 12:30 a.m., Denise was in the waiting room with her family, the Berrys, and Poppy, when Mandi and her family entered the emergency room. The two girls hugged each other as Mandi asked, "How's Todd doing?"

Denise replied, "So far, all tests have been negative, but the doctors don't know why he's showing signs of paralysis."

Mandi remarked, "I just heard about the accident and asked Mom and Dad if they would bring me here."

Denise replied, "Thank you for coming. It looks like Todd's friends are concerned about him."

Mandi added, "Denise, we are concerned about you, too. You and Todd have become close friends over the past few months."

Denise answered, "That's true."

Mandi continued, "Please call on me if I can help you in any way. You are one of my best friends."

Denise replied, "Thank you, Mandi."

While they were talking, one of the doctors entered the room. He told them, "We can't find any reason for him to be paralyzed. Hopefully, it is just temporary. Something happened during the accident that caused it. It may be from the trauma of the accident itself."

He continued, "We hope he'll start getting feeling in his extremities shortly. The next few hours are critical. Nerve damage heals very slowly, so it is going to take some time for him to get completely well if there is damage to the spinal cord. I've explained this to him, so he knows what to expect."

The doctor continued, "We are placing him in intensive care for now as a precaution. Are there any questions?"

Coach Berry asked, "If there is no nerve damage, how quickly can we expect him to recover?"

The doctor replied, "If there is no nerve damage, we could see him get his feeling back as soon as forty-eight hours or so."

Coach Berry told everyone, "Let's pray that the injury is only minor."

Denise asked her parents if she could stay at the hospital the rest of the night.

The doctor told her, "There's not anything you can do for him if you stay here. I recommend you say good night to him and come back tomorrow. We want him to get as much rest as possible tonight while we watch him closely. You'll be more important to him when he is awake."

Denise went to Todd's room, took his limp hand and rubbed it. She could barely keep the tears from her eyes when she pleaded with him, "Please Todd, promise me you won't give up. After talking to the doctors, I feel like you're going to be okay. I love you, and I want you to get well. Will you promise me you won't give up?"

Todd didn't have much feeling, but he knew his heart was beating fast. He was very lucky to have such a beautiful person love him. He slowly answered, "Don't worry...I'm a competitor. I'll...be okay."

Denise visited with Mandi and her parents before she left for home. It meant a great deal for her friends to come to Dallas to check on her and Todd.

It wasn't easy for Denise to leave Todd by himself, but she knew the doctor was right. She would be with him tomorrow as much as the intensive care unit would allow her.

Denise didn't sleep much that night. She couldn't forget how limp Todd's hand felt in hers. She prayed, "Lord, please see Todd through this accident. He's a good person. Just let him get well and be normal again. Please!"

As she prayed for Todd's recovery, she slowly slipped into a restless sleep. Thoughts continued to haunt her as if they were bad dreams. Throughout the night, she tossed and turned as she dreamed about the accident.

Saturday morning, the Pooles were at the hospital by 9 a.m. Denise and her mother were permitted to see Todd for only a few minutes. The intensive care unit was very strict on their visitation time limits.

When Todd saw her he complained, "My hands tingle. They're driving me crazy."

A nurse who was standing near-by told Denise, "That's a good, positive sign."

Denise replied, "Oh...thank goodness." She looked at Todd and continued, "Did you rest much last night?"

He answered, "They said I did, but I sure had some bad dreams. I can't figure out what happened, and besides, I have a terrible headache. What about my car? Have you seen it?"

Denise shook her head and answered, "No. I haven't taken time to go look at it. I'm not too sure I want to see it."

Denise wanted to ask him about his drinking, but she wanted to remain positive. She knew they could discuss that issue at a later time.

It was several hours before Denise and her parents could talk to a doctor. Finally, a neurologist visited with them in the waiting room and told them, "The tingling in his extremities is a good sign. After viewing all of the tests, we feel as though he should have a full recovery. He is in excellent physical condition, and that is a major plus for him."

As they were talking, Coach Berry and Poppy came into the room. After listening to the doctor and visiting with Todd, Poppy told Denise, "I think it is just a matter of time before Todd is up and at'em."

CHAPTER 12

Sunday morning, the doctor sat beside Todd and said, "Todd, you are a very lucky young man. Your reflexes are much improved, and that is good. Do you have any pain?"

Todd replied, "Just this terrible headache. I can't seem to get rid of it."

The doctor responded, "The headache must be from the whiplash. All of your tests are negative. Again, you're very lucky."

Todd nodded, "I know. I never thought about how good it feels to move my arms and legs...just being able to scratch an itch...Man!... By the way, what caused me to be paralyzed?"

The doctor answered, "In the past, we have had people paralyzed from trauma. Yours was probably caused from a spinal cord concussion, much like getting a brain concussion while playing football."

Todd said, "I've had my bell rung while I was making tackles, but never anything like this. Do you think I'll get to play football again?"

The doctor thought a moment, and answered, "Not anytime soon. I would definitely have a thorough physical before playing again. In fact, I would think seriously about ever playing football again."

Todd asked, "If there is no damage, what is the danger?"

The doctor answered, "The danger is the unknown. What if there is something we haven't found. You may have absolutely nothing wrong with you, but is it worth the risk of receiving a permanent injury?"

Todd thought, then asked, "So the decision will be mine to make, right?"

"That's right! If you really want to play again, you need to sit out at least a year. By that time, you should know if there are any problems. Hopefully everything is going to be just fine. For the time being, I'm going to put you in a private room."

"I'm getting out of ICU?"

"That's right! However, you still need to be very careful when you walk. Don't go anywhere without someone walking with you."

Todd replied, "Don't worry! I haven't gotten much of my strength back, yet."

The doctor smiled and said, "It won't be long."

That afternoon, Todd was placed in a private room. While he was alone, he reflected on the events of the past weekend, *"What will people think? How will my friends and teammates react to my getting drunk?"*

He was upset about wrecking his new car, but he was more embarrassed because of the drinking. He thought, *"Why did I have to make such a fool of myself?"*

In the quietness of his room, he tried to visualize going back to school. He sure hated to face everyone, after such an embarrassing episode. He wondered, *"Will everyone stare at me?"*

He had to get these depressing ideas out of his head. He raised the head of his bed so he could look out the big window in his room that faced downtown.

Downtown Dallas was awesome. There was always so much going on in a large city like this.

His thoughts changed when he thought about what Coach Berry had asked him just last Monday, *"Have you thought anymore about the commitment you made to God?"*

He asked himself, *"Has money changed me?"*

When someone knocked on the door, he turned and said, "Come on in!"

Denise looked inside before entering the room, and asked, "Todd, is that you?"

"Sure, come in!"

"When did they move you?"

"About an hour ago."

"How do you feel?"

"Better! A lot better, but I still have a headache."

"Are you able to move?"

"I have to be cautious. The doctor doesn't want me to go anywhere by myself."

"Thank goodness! I'm so relieved. Todd, I was so worried about you."

Todd paused before continuing, "Denise…I owe you an apology. I'm sorry I put you through this."

"I wish we could have talked before you left town. What made you leave town, anyway?"

"I guess the thought of you being with someone else rattled me."

Denise asked, "May I sit on the bed?"

"Sure!"

She sat on the side of the hospital bed, facing Todd.

He looked into her dark brown eyes and asked, "Denise, have I changed since I got that money?"

She replied, "I don't think so. Being jealous has nothing to do with money."

Todd didn't like the word "jealous." However, that was what happened. He got jealous when he saw Darren's car at Denise's house.

He gently took her hand and commented, "Denise, don't let me change. I don't want money if it is going to make me different."

They looked at each other as he continued, "I almost killed myself this weekend…that's scary."

Denise asked, "Todd, you're not going to become a drinker, are you?"

Todd never hesitated as he answered, "No way! I was miserable. I couldn't control my car or anything else. It was a horrible feeling."

"Todd, promise me that you will talk to me before doing anything foolish again."

"I promise. I hope I've learned my lesson. Denise, when you came in, I was trying to figure out where my life is headed. Coach

Berry asked me last week about my commitment to God, and I don't know…I'm sure He has a plan for me, but…I don't know what it is."

Denise replied, "I've prayed very hard for your recovery this weekend, and I believe He has answered that prayer. He will show you when the time is right."

Clay knocked on the door and stuck his head in and asked, "Hey bud, you okay?"

Todd smiled and answered, "Sure, come in!"

Clay, Cindy, and Stanley entered the room and encircled the hospital bed. Cindy had several "GET WELL" balloons, which she tied to the foot of Todd's bed.

Clay's first question was, "You going to be able to use your arms and legs again?"

Cindy snapped, "Clay!"

Everyone laughed as Todd replied, "Yep! The doctor told me this morning that I should be okay. It may take me a while, but I'm going to be fine."

Clay asked, "What about football? Are you going to be able to play again?"

Todd answered, "The doctor said that I need to sit out at least a year before playing again. He really doesn't want me to ever play football, but he said that would be my decision."

Clay continued, "Is there a reason he doesn't want you to play football?"

Denise quickly asked, "Hey, that's right! Why doesn't he want you to play?"

Todd looked at everyone before answering, "He told me that there wasn't any damage to my neck or spinal cord, but after an injury like this one, he just doesn't recommend a contact sport."

Clay commented, "Todd, you'll have to make your neck stronger, you know, like those pro football players."

He flexed his muscles to make his neck look larger, when the doctor entered the room.

The four teenagers laughed at Clay when he quickly sat in a chair. The doctor commented, "Well, looks like you're beginning to feel better."

When everyone had stopped laughing at Clay, Denise asked, "When will Todd get to go home?"

The doctor replied, "He's doing just fine. If there are no complications, we will probably release him Tuesday. Right now, I don't foresee any problems. He's healthy and in excellent condition."

Denise responded, "Great! I'll get Mother or Dad to come with me to pick him up."

· · · · · · · ●· · · · · · · · ·

Tuesday afternoon, Don and Bettie Poole helped Denise bring Todd home. He was still weak, but seemed to get stronger each day.

Poppy was waiting for his grandson when he got out of the car. Todd walked cautiously to the front door with Denise on one side and Mr. Poole on the other.

The old man held the door open for his grandson as he entered the house. Don Poole helped Todd into the bedroom.

Todd commented, "It's sure great to be home again."

Bettie Poole asked, "Poppy, is there anything you need?"

Poppy answered, "I don't think so. I've been to the grocery store. I think we have everything we need."

Bettie continued, "If you think of anything, call us and we will get it for you."

Poppy nodded, "Thank you. That's nice of you to offer."

Denise mentioned to Poppy, "The doctor told Todd that he has to do his therapy every day." She looked at Todd and continued, "He knows what he has to do. He may need you to see that he does it."

Todd remarked, "Don't worry, I will do my exercises. I want to get back to normal as soon as I can."

He missed the rest of the school week, but worked extremely hard on his rehabilitation.

Todd was able to return to school the following Monday. He was just as self-conscious as he had been following his kidnapping in the late fall.

Physically, Todd was feeling almost normal, but he was still weak. The doctor told him that his therapy would have him back to normal in a few weeks.

The school year was almost over, and graduation was just around the corner. Todd was beginning to experience periods of depression. Denise tried to get him to talk about it, but he didn't express his feelings very well when he felt like this.

On Thursday night, Todd was feeling down, so he walked to the football field. The doctor had told him to walk as much as possible, and without his car, he seemed to be walking quite often.

Denise called to talk to Todd, but Poppy told her he was walking. She knew he would probably go to the football stadium, so she drove there to see him.

She got out of the car and walked into the empty stadium. When she entered the gate, she saw him walking on the field. Denise watched him for several minutes.

Todd had walked to the spot where he threw the touchdown pass to Stanley in the championship game in November. She watched him as he stepped through the play in slow motion. He then acted like he threw the ball, which Stanley caught for the touchdown.

Denise couldn't help but cheer for him. She knew he would be embarrassed when he realized she was watching him go through the motions of playing football.

He quickly turned around and asked, "How long have you been here?"

"Just a few minutes. Nice pass!"

Todd grinned as he started walking toward her. They met in the middle of the field. They looked at each other for a moment and gave each other a kiss.

The sun was below the horizon, and daylight was fading quickly. It was late April, but the air began to cool rapidly when the sun disappeared below the horizon.

Todd took Denise's hand while they walked toward the end zone. Denise asked, "What's bothering you?"

"I don't know. School is almost over, and I don't know what the future holds."

"What do you mean?"

"Well, I probably won't get to play football next season. I wonder if I should work...and not go to college?"

Denise snapped, "You *will* go to school! Money is no issue for you, and the longer you wait, the harder it'll be to finish."

"Yeah, I guess you're right. However, you know I'm going to miss being with you."

"We won't be that far apart...just about an hour's drive. What's really bothering you?"

Todd knew he couldn't fool Denise. They had only been dating for about four months, but she knew him like a book.

Todd and Denise walked to the goalpost, where they sat on the ground. Todd leaned against it while Denise sat on the ground facing him. He thought awhile, and finally said, "I don't know what I want to do for a career. I had visions of playing professional football, but that's not being realistic."

I made a commitment to God to do what He wanted me to do, but I guess I must be missing something. I don't know what it is He wants me to do."

Denise asked, "Have you prayed about it?"

"Yes, but maybe I'm not praying right."

Denise replied, "You have to have faith that you will know when the time is right."

"I've thought about everything He might ask me to do; preach, but I can't see me preaching. Be a Missionary? I don't think so!"

"There are other things."

"Like what?"

"There are Christian lawyers, doctors...you can be a Christian in any field. What do you want in a life?"

Todd responded, "I want to be a good husband and father."

"What kind of career?"

"I really don't know. I know I don't want to sit behind a desk. I want to be active. I want to do something that has meaning. Take Coach Berry for example. Where would I be if it weren't for him? Wait a minute...that's it! That's it! I can be a coach."

Denise was surprised. She had never thought about Todd coaching. She asked, "Are you sure?"

Todd replied, "I think so. I believe I would enjoy coaching. I would be active, involved in young lives…I think that's it!"

Denise could see an immediate change in Todd's attitude. She knew she would have to think about this. Would she want to be married to a coach? She asked, "Would you like to talk to Coach Berry about it?"

"Hey, that's a good idea. Would you like to take me to his house?"

"Sure, let's go."

Todd took Denise's hand, and they walked to her car. He was still stiff from the accident, so she drove slowly to the Berry's house.

Todd rang the doorbell and waited for someone to answer it. Beth Berry opened the door and exclaimed, "Denise! Todd! Would you like to come in?"

Todd answered, "Sure. Is Coach Berry home?"

Beth replied, "He's in the den with the children. Come on in."

The two teenagers followed her to the back of the house where Coach Berry was just getting up. He said, "Have a seat. What brings you two over?"

Todd answered, "Denise and I were at the football field tonight, and we were discussing the question you asked me last Monday, about my commitment to God. Well, I may have come up with an answer."

Coach Berry said, "Great, what have you decided?"

Todd replied, "I think I would like to coach."

After a moment of silence, Coach Berry responded, "You would make a good one. What made you decide on coaching?"

Denise watched Todd as he seemed to get excited when he talked about his future. There appeared to be a burden lifted from his shoulders as he talked about coaching.

Todd answered, "Denise and I were discussing the commitment that I couldn't seem to find an answer to, when she asked me what I wanted to do. I told her how much you had done for me, and that seemed to trigger the idea of coaching."

Coach Berry looked at Denise and asked, "How do you feel about Todd coaching?"

She replied, "I never have thought about it before. I agree with you; I think he would make an excellent coach. I want him to be happy in whatever he does."

Todd asked, "What do I need to be a coach?"

Coach Berry told him, "You'll have to get a teacher's certificate in some teaching field, and then you must decide what you want to coach and at what level."

Todd quickly answered, "Football! I want to be a football coach."

Coach Berry then told Todd, "I'm glad you have set your goal to be a coach, but remember, there is always the possibility you may want to change your mind, and there is nothing wrong with that. The main thing to keep in mind is you have to do what will make you and your wife happy."

Todd answered, "Right, but at least this is a start."

Coach Berry replied, "That's right. There's always a need for young Christian coaches."

Beth asked, "Would either of you like something to drink?"

Both Denise and Todd accepted a soft drink, as they talked about Todd's career and future.

When they left the Berry's house, Denise was beginning to feel better about Todd's decision. At first, she had been surprised, but now she was beginning to understand his feelings.

· · · · · · · · ● · · · · · · · · ·

Todd got his car out of the repair shop on the first Friday afternoon of May. He then went to Clay's house to pick him up. They drove to the local hangout where they ran into Stanley.

They sat in a booth and discussed the last few weeks of the school year.

Todd said, "When I picked up my mail today, I got my last test results back from the doctor. Everything is great; however, he doesn't want me to play football next year."

Stanley asked, "What are you going to do?"

Todd answered, "I'm going to school, train and get ready for the following season."

Stanley asked Clay, "What are you going to study?"

Clay replied, "Besides football?"

"Yeah! What are you interested in?"

Clay said, "I haven't really thought about it that much. I might be a coach, like Todd. What are you going to do?"

Stanley remarked, "I'm joining the Army in June. After that I may come back and go to college."

As they were talking, two of the guys Todd drank beer with before the accident entered the room.

One of them by the name of Jack said to Todd, "Want to go have a beer tonight?"

Clay and Stanley watched as Todd turned red in the face. He got up and said, "Jack, I will tell you one time, and one time only. *Never* mention the word "beer" around me again! Do you understand?"

Jack could see that Todd was upset. He reluctantly backed off, "Okay...Okay! Forget it."

As Jack backed off, the other one, Carl, commented to Todd, "What's bothering you?"

Todd snapped, "I don't think I need to answer that!"

As they stood glaring at each other, Clay got up and stepped in front of Todd and said, "I think it would be a good idea if you two left!"

Clay and Todd were large football players and in excellent physical condition, and as Stanley rose beside his teammates, Carl and Jack decided it might be a good idea to leave before trouble started.

When Jack turned to leave, he mentioned, "You should learn to handle your beer."

Clay grabbed Todd as he started toward the two former schoolmates. He commented, "Whoa, Todd! It's not worth it!"

Todd stopped and replied, "You're right. It's not worth getting in trouble over them."

After averting a near incident, Clay asked, "Why did you get so upset? You know you can't afford to get hurt, especially in a fight."

Todd answered, "I almost killed myself on that stuff! I don't want to be reminded of it!"

When the three teammates all sat down and finished their drinks, Clay thought he needed to change the subject, so he asked Todd, "What are you and Denise doing tonight?"

"We're renting a movie and are going to watch it at her house. What about you?"

"Cindy and I are going to a movie downtown."

Todd asked, "Why don't you two come to Denise's house. She told me to invite you if I wanted to."

"Sure! What time?"

"About 7:30. Her parents are taking us out to eat first. We will watch the movie when we get back."

Clay responded, "Okay! See you then."

Clay and Todd said good-bye to Stanley and left. When Todd dropped Clay at his house, Clay remarked, "I'll bring the booze!"

"What?"

"Kidding! Just kidding!"

CHAPTER 13

When Todd and Clay left the weight room, Clay asked, "Are you going to the awards ceremony tonight?"

Todd replied, "Sure, I got an invitation Monday to go. What about you; did you get an invitation?"

"Yeah, I'm going. I got one Monday, also."

The ceremony was to award scholarships and recognize the honor students for the year. The school has always had the event at night, so parents and family members could share in the awards. Invitations were sent to the families of the students who were going to receive the awards. The students usually dressed nicely if they were getting an honor.

Clay asked, "What are you going to wear?"

Todd responded, "I think I'll wear my blue sport coat."

"You wearing a tie?"

"Yeah, I think they want us to. What are you going to wear?"

"I guess I'll wear a tie, too. What kind of award is Denise getting tonight?"

"I'm not sure. She is one of the top honor students, but she doesn't know which one. It's really been close between her and Mandi all year."

"Are you two going together?"

"I'm picking her up about 6:30."

As Clay turned to leave, he commented, "Okay, I'll see both of you tonight."

Todd picked up Denise at 6:30. She was beautiful in her dress. Her tan arms and neck stood out next to the light blue material. It fit her sleek figure perfectly. He followed behind her and watched as she gracefully seated herself in his car.

As he left the driveway, he murmured in her ear, "You sure look nice, tonight."

She replied, "Well, thank you. So do you."

When they arrived at the school auditorium, they checked in with the school sponsors and sat with Clay and Cindy, who were already in their places. After Todd and Denise settled in their seats, he watched Poppy walk in and take a seat.

Todd could remember when he was almost embarrassed for the old man to be at his activities. Now he had found an attraction toward him, a love that had grown during the past year.

Shortly, the ceremony started. Clay and Todd were recognized for receiving football scholarships at Texas Eastern University.

Denise received a small scholarship from a local women's group and another one from a local service club.

Todd received a small scholarship for citizenship, presented by a civic club in the community.

The high school principal, Mr. Black, gave out the last scholarship for citizenship as well as a scholastic achievement award, which went to Denise.

Finally, the highlight of the ceremony was the graduating honor students. Pat Deen had the fourth highest grade-point average. Carol Jones had the third highest average.

Anticipation was building for the top two students. Todd noticed Denise was growing tense as the time grew near. Mr. Black announced, "The salutatorian for this year's class is...Denise Poole!"

Denise rose and went to the stage. Mr. Black placed a satin neck-sash around her neck that had "salutatorian" printed on it.

"The valedictorian is...Mandi Stowe!"

Everyone stood and applauded as Mandi approached the stage. Denise was disappointed about being runner-up, but she was proud for Mandi, one of her best friends. They had always been close to each other.

When Mandi received her satin neck-sash, she and Denise smiled and hugged each other.

Todd was proud of Denise for her achievements. She had worked hard for her honors and had overcome a lot of adversities in her final year of high school. First came the kidnapping, then the broken leg, and finally Todd's wreck early in April.

Following the ceremony, the school officials held a reception for the recipients and their families. Todd and Denise stood together as people congratulated them.

Coach Berry and Beth stopped to speak to them. Coach Berry told them, "I'm proud of both of you. You deserve the honors you received tonight."

Todd and Denise responded together, "Thank you!"

Beth commented, "You two sure make a nice looking couple. It's rewarding to see good kids get honors."

Coach Berry and Todd shook hands while Beth and Denise hugged each other.

When the reception was over, Todd and Denise left in Todd's car. He asked, "Mind if we go to the football field?"

"No. It would be fine with me."

Denise could tell Todd was beginning to get sentimental as the evening drew to an end. The young couple got out of the car and walked hand and hand to the field.

Todd stopped and looked at the dimly lit field.

Denise asked, "Anything wrong?"

"No! I was just thinking how much has happened this year. When football season started, I just barely knew you. Now, you're the most important person in my life. I was very proud of you tonight."

Denise was silent for a moment, then she agreed, "A lot has happened this year."

They had slowly moved to mid-field as they talked.

Todd looked at the rising moon. It was just coming up on the eastern horizon; it was a gibbous moon, much like the one in November when they had won the championship.

They put their arms around each other and stood quietly in the middle of the field. Todd whispered, "I wish you could have met my parents. I know they would have been proud of you, just like I am."

Denise laid her head on his strong shoulders and said, "I know I would have loved them; I'm sure they are proud of you."

After they kissed each other, they stood in the moonlight, talking about the past year.

Denise had never mentioned the incident about how Darren had gotten fresh with her to Todd, but tonight she wondered what would have happened if the altercation hadn't occurred.

She knew she most likely would have been kidnapped, but Todd wouldn't have been there to rescue her. It scared her to think about being kidnapped alone. Several things could have happened to her, and all of them would have been bad.

She wondered, "Would I have been this close to Todd if that incident hadn't occurred?"

She didn't think so, but that was a question she would never be able to answer.

Todd was right. A lot had happened this school year.

· · · · · · · ● · · · · · · ·

Graduation day finally arrived. Several of Todd's family members were coming to see him graduate. He hadn't seen some of his aunts and uncles since he had lived in their homes. One was coming from northern Oklahoma, while the other aunt was driving from south Texas.

He was glad they were coming to see him finish his high school career.

As a graduation gift, the Pooles were paying for Todd, Denise, Clay, and Cindy to go in a limousine to a large graduation party in Dallas. They would be out all night. Todd knew he wouldn't be able to spend much time with his family, but he felt as though they would understand.

Todd was getting dressed when his family arrived. When he met them, they all hugged him and commented about how much he had grown and how he had matured physically. Several of his little cousins teased with him as he finished getting dressed. He visited with them until it was time to leave.

When Todd arrived at the football stadium, Clay asked him, "Where is Denise?"

Todd replied, "She should be here anytime now. Her parents are bringing her."

Clay asked, "Is the limo still picking us up around 9:30?"

Todd answered, "Yep. It'll pick us up at Denise's house. I have asked Denise to go to Poppy's house after the ceremony to meet my family. We should get to the Poole's house about the time the limo arrives."

Clay responded, "I understand. I think it's great that they are getting to meet her. In fact, I would like to meet them myself. What if Cindy and I picked you two up, then we could go to the Poole's house together in my car."

Todd continued, "Great, we shouldn't be at Poppy's too long. My aunts and uncles have a long way to drive, so they have to leave fairly early."

Clay commented, "You like to show her off, don't you?"

Todd smiled and said, "I want her to meet my family because Poppy is the only one she knows."

Clay responded, "I know they'll like her."

Todd turned when he heard Denise call his name. She told him, "I put some gifts in your car for some of my friends. Is that okay?"

"Sure, did you lock it?"

Denise acknowledged, "Yes."

Todd told her, "I'm glad you're going to Poppy's after graduation. I'm anxious for some of my family to meet you."

She smiled, "Good! I'm looking forward to meeting them, too. Have they arrived yet?"

"Yeah. They got here about an hour ago."

Denise asked, "Are Cindy and Clay going to Poppy's after the ceremony?"

"Yeah. They're going to pick us up at Poppy's house about 9:15."

Everyone reacted when Mr. Thompson, one of the senior sponsors said, "Everyone needs to line up. You know where to go!"

Todd asked, "Are you nervous about your speech?"

Denise answered, "I was okay earlier, but the closer it comes to the speech, the more it begins to bother me."

Before Denise left for the front of the line, they hugged each other. Todd told her, "Good luck!"

She replied, "Thanks!"

As they lined up, Todd couldn't believe he was finishing his high school career. He thought, "All of the challenges and tests are finished."

Normally, Todd would be sitting close to Denise, but tonight, being an honor student, she would be one of the first to enter the temporary stage set up on the football field.

At last the music, "Pomp and Circumstance," started, and the line started to move. Todd's heart began to speed up. He realized, "This is it. Graduation!"

He looked into the stands to find Poppy and the rest of his family. He thought, "That's strange. I never thought about how many people were in the stands during a football game, but since I have my family sitting in them, they look big. I wonder where they're sitting?"

When he entered the stage area, he heard one of his cousins call his name, and he was able to locate them. He smiled as he thought, "It's great to have my family here to see me graduate. I wish they could have seen me play football."

After everyone was seated, Denise approached the podium. Todd got nervous when she spoke into the microphone. He could barely listen to her for thinking about how lucky he was to have her for a girlfriend.

At this point, he didn't want to think about the future any more because he wanted to remember each moment of the ceremony.

Finally, the time came for the seniors to receive their diplomas. He knew Perry would be one of the latter ones to cross the stage. He watched his classmates get their diplomas and shake hands with the president of the local school board.

First to cross was Mandi, then Denise. He watched Clay take his diploma, then Pat received his. Todd thought, "It won't be long now."

Soon his row stood. He couldn't believe the emotion that filled him. He tried to smile, but the muscles in his face wouldn't cooperate.

He was now next in line, then he heard, "Philip Todd Perry."

He proudly walked across the stage and took the diploma with his left hand and gave a firm handshake with his right hand. He thought, "Wow! I finally got it."

He wanted to remember his parents on this occasion. As he left the center of the stage, he held his diploma up and looked skyward to recognize his parents, Sherry and Philip Perry.

Denise saw what Todd did and knew what he was thinking. A tear rolled down her cheek when she saw him make the gesture toward his parents. She knew they would be proud of his achievements.

Before long, the graduation exercise was over, and the school song was played for the last time. Suddenly the air above them was full of graduation caps.

All of the seniors began to congratulate each other. Todd could not remember hugging so many classmates. Some had tears of joy in their eyes, but everyone was excited about the great accomplishment of completing high school.

Family and friends soon entered the field and gave their congratulations to all of the seniors.

Don Poole shook Todd's hand, then Bettie hugged him. Mr. Poole whispered in Todd's ear, "Have a good time tonight, but *do be careful*. You two are very special to us."

Todd wondered if the "be careful" meant not to drink. That was something that he knew he wouldn't do.

Todd looked him in the eyes with a newfound confidence and replied, "Don't worry, sir. We will have a great time, and I can assure you we *will* be careful."

Todd felt his robe being pulled from the rear. As he looked around, he saw his little cousins trying to get his attention. He picked both of them up at the same time and said to the Pooles, "Mr. and Mrs. Poole, I would like for you to meet my cousins, Candy and Tommy."

Soon his aunts found him in the mass of graduates. He introduced them to the Pooles, "These are my mother's sisters.

Elizabeth, who drove down from Tulsa, and Jeanie came all the way from Houston."

Mr. Poole shook their hands as Bettie spoke to both of the little ones. Todd put his small cousins down when he saw Denise approaching.

Denise went to Todd and gave him a big hug. He told her, "Your speech was great." He then introduced her to each of his family members.

The gathering on the field was soon over as seniors scattered for the last time. Todd and Denise went to Poppy's house where Todd changed into more casual clothes. After Todd changed clothes, he and Denise visited until Clay and Cindy arrived.

Todd introduced the two of them to everyone, then he began to say his goodbyes. He couldn't leave until he had hugged and thanked his aunts and uncles for coming at this special time in his life.

The limousine was waiting when the two young couples arrived at the Poole's house. Denise had to change clothes before they left. Todd and Clay kept looking out the window at the long white car parked in the front of the house.

Clay remarked, "The last time I rode in a vehicle that long, it was called a bus."

Todd smiled and replied, "I'm anxious to see the inside of it."

"Yeah, me too. I've never seen one before."

"I haven't either."

As they admired the limousine, the two girls came into the room. Denise exclaimed, "I'm ready! Let's go!"

Clay stated, "The last one in is a—"

Cindy snapped, "Clay!"

Clay stopped and apologized, "Sorry."

Don and Bettie Poole went with the two couples to the car and watched them as they admired the long vehicle. One by one they got in and closed the door. The Pooles stood and waved as the limousine drove off.

The four graduates joked and played with the gadgets in the car as it headed for Dallas. Soon they were in the big city and arrived at a nightclub where a large number of seniors were celebrating their graduation night.

They hadn't been at the party very long before Todd became aware that most of the people at the party were drinking, and some of them fairly heavily.

The two couples spent most of the time with each other. However, there were other seniors from Wills that had come to the same party, and they visited from time to time.

After Todd and Denise had danced together several times, Todd asked Cindy for a dance, and Clay danced with Denise. While Denise was dancing with Clay, she noticed a stranger in a green shirt wink at her. She immediately ignored his gaze.

Denise didn't mention the incident to Todd after the two couples returned to their table. She had almost forgotten about it when she and Cindy went to the restroom together. When they started back to their table, some one grabbed her by the arm and said, "Hey cutie, how about a dance?"

Denise could smell alcohol on his breath when he spoke to her. She calmly told him, "Forget it! I'm with someone else!"

She jerked her arm away from him and started to the table. She quickly realized that he had been the one who winked at her earlier.

Cindy asked, "Who was that?"

Denise replied, "I don't know and don't care to find out. Don't say anything to Todd or Clay about this. I'm afraid it might cause trouble."

Cindy responded, "Okay, if you say so."

The band started a slow number, and Todd took Denise's hand and led her to the dance floor. He asked, "Is something wrong?"

Denise answered, "No. Uh…why?"

He commented, "You looked upset when you came back to the table."

Denise, trying to prevent trouble, uttered, "Uh, you know what it's like when there is a line at the restroom. It's frustrating to waste time waiting in a line."

After having some snacks, Todd and Denise moved onto the dance floor, again. As they danced smoothly across the floor, Denise noticed the guy who had made the advance toward her coming in their direction. His approach unsettled her. When she saw him coming, she turned and told Todd, "Let's go to the table!"

Todd asked, "What's wrong with you?"

"Nothing! I just want to sit down for a minute!"

Todd replied, "Okay, but something's bothering—"

Before he could finish his statement, the intruder had stopped her and said, "I think it's about time you danced with a real man!"

When the agitator moved towards Denise, Todd grabbed him by the front of the shirt with his left hand and almost lifted him off the floor. Instead of hitting him, Todd, with his fist doubled-up, looked him in his eyes and said, "Fellow, I'll tell you one time, so you better listen carefully. If you ever touch her again, I'll spread your nose all over your face!"

Several of the guy's buddies started toward Todd, but the muscular, six-foot-two, two hundred twenty-five pound Clay Comer stepped in front of them and said, "I haven't had any fun in a long time. Now which one of you fellows wants to be the first to come forward?"

The group slowly backed away from the grinning Clay. The intruder Todd was holding wanted to save face, but his feet were barely touching the floor. He muttered, "Okay, okay!...I hear you! Put me down!"

Todd released him with a push and watched as he fell to the floor.

Clay, who was enjoying intimidating the others, said, "Ahh shucks! What a shame! The last time someone fooled with his girlfriend, *he* wound up in the hospital. This guy is really lucky, tonight!"

The group sheepishly returned to their tables without saying anything to the grinning Clay.

Denise quickly grabbed Todd's arm and pulled him to the table and said, "Maybe we should go!"

Todd replied, "We're not going to let those drunks run us off."

Clay's intimidating must have worked because no one bothered them after the incident.

Denise was visibly shaken by the near fight, but Todd's ability to protect her made her feel secure. It was a good feeling.

Around 3 a.m., Todd and Denise asked Cindy and Clay if they wanted to go downtown; they quickly agreed.

The limousine drove them to Reunion Tower, the large building in downtown Dallas that has the ball on top. They rode the elevator to the restaurant at the top of the tower. They ordered a dessert and observed the city of Dallas as the room revolved.

By five o'clock, when the two couples were about to get in the limousine and start home, Todd pulled Clay aside, and asked, "Do you remember the park we passed at the lake, when I had my eighteenth birthday party?"

"Yeah. Why?"

"Why don't we take the girls there and watch the sunrise?"

"Hey, that's a great idea! I'll draw a map for the driver. Don't tell the girls."

When the driver turned off the main road on the way home, Cindy immediately asked, "Hey, where's he taking us?"

Clay told her, "Don't worry about it."

Denise gave Todd a puzzled look. He whispered in her ear, "It's a surprise."

When the driver turned into the small park, the sky was just beginning to glow with the approaching dawn.

Both couples were exhausted from being up all night, but that seemed to make this time together even more special.

The two couples walked to different places. Clay and Cindy found a grassy area and sat down. Cindy leaned against Clay as they faced the calm water and orange sky.

Todd and Denise found a picnic table and sat on top of it. Denise commented, "The water is so smooth."

The reflection of the sky on the water was breathtaking. Todd kissed Denise warmly. She put both arms around his neck in response to his kiss.

The lake setting was so romantic, and they were totally absorbed with each other. Denise looked into Todd's eyes and whispered, "Todd, I love you very much. I can't imagine what it would be like without you. I do appreciate how you handled that incident tonight. There could have been a fight. Thank you."

Todd, ignored her praise and replied, "Just think, we hardly knew each other when school started this year. Now, we are very dependent on each other. I am sure glad you broke up with Darren."

When the sun peeked above the horizon, Denise's eyes began to sparkle. As they walked back to the limousine arm in arm, Todd told her, "I feel very lucky to be with you. At the beginning of the school year, I didn't think about girls at all, much less dating someone."

Denise wondered, "*Should I tell him about Darren? No. I don't think it would do any good. It's best to forget about that incident and get on with our lives.*"

Denise stopped, and looked at Todd as she spoke, "God had a special plan that we didn't realize."

She thought about the incident with Darren and how Todd came into her life at the right time, then she continued, "God brought you into my life in a special way, and I'm very thankful that he did."

Todd, not knowing that she was referring to Darren, still agreed with her about God bringing them together. He commented, "I didn't even know God until I met you. Now, I feel like he has guided you into my life for a reason. I just hope He will continue to watch our relationship."

Denise agreed, "Me too."

When they arrived at the car, the driver of the car was asleep behind the steering wheel. He jumped when Todd hollered, "Hey Clay, it's time to go!"

CHAPTER 14

Todd got out of his red car and walked into Poppy's house, where he would spend the summer. Things just weren't the same since Poppy's death in late February. Todd reminisced about Poppy's last heart attack. He had gone quickly, but Todd had been able to visit with him before he died.

He would never forget Poppy's last words, "I've loved you as if you were my own son. I hope you'll take care of Denise. You two make such a nice couple."

The only family Todd had left was his aunts and uncles on his mother's side, and he hadn't seen them since his high school graduation last May.

He walked around the house, thumbed through some of his wild west novels, placed them back on the bookshelves, and walked to his room. He looked at some of Denise's pictures and was grateful he would be able to spend time with her this summer.

It was Friday afternoon, and Denise would be home shortly. She had invited him to eat with her family and help her unpack. He had talked to her almost daily when they were at school, but he hadn't seen her in over two weeks because of final exams. It was hard to go that long without being with her.

As he gazed at his favorite senior portrait of Denise, he felt some of the same emotion he had when he kissed her the first time. She was a special person, and he missed her tremendously.

Todd sat down and thought about his summer job, working in construction. He and Clay had decided to work together during the summer. He had invested much of his money and didn't have to work to make a living now; however, he knew working would help him stay in shape for football.

They would start to work on Monday, but first he would have to get his phone reconnected. After Poppy's death, Todd had left the electricity on because he came home as often as possible to see Denise. He had disconnected the phone because he wouldn't need it until he finished his freshman year of college and returned for summer vacation.

It felt good to get the first year of college behind him. College life was completely different from high school. College students had to answer for themselves.

Todd's coaches kept a close eye on their athletes, but other than that they were on their own. That wasn't as big a change for Todd as it had been for some of the other freshmen. Since he had moved to Wills to live with Poppy, Todd had been free to make decisions for himself.

After Todd cleaned up, he drove to the Poole's house. Denise had returned from college earlier in the afternoon and was still unpacking when he arrived. She met him at the front door and hugged him. They quickly kissed and went into the house. Don and Bettie Poole were also glad to see Todd. They almost considered him a member of their family.

After supper, Todd and Denise finished unpacking her boxes and drove to the football stadium, where they climbed to the top of the stands and sat down. It was apparent they both had matured considerably during the past year.

Being separated so much made them appreciate the time they shared together. Denise could tell that Todd had gained some extra weight during the past year. The college training program had helped him develop physically.

Denise planned to attend a small community college this summer to finish some of her required courses. She had been in school every semester since her high school graduation. This would help her finish college early. Going to the community college would also enable her to be with Todd all summer.

As the sun set behind some gray clouds, Todd asked, "Have you registered for summer school yet?"

"No, I'll do that Monday and start classes on Tuesday. Do you start work Monday?"

"Yeah. Clay and I have to be at work at seven o'clock."

"Isn't that a little early?"

"Yeah, but we get off work early."

"Well, that's one way to look at it. What will you two be doing?"

"We'll be helping electricians wire some new buildings. They say it'll be hot."

Denise paused, then said, "Todd, I sure have missed you the last two weeks. It was hard to study. I wanted to call you more than what I did."

"I know that feeling. I was afraid some of those rich guys would be taking you out if I wasn't with you."

"Well, I did have several offers, but I turned them down…you know I had to study!"

Denise smiled as she teased him. Todd tried to smile, but the thought of her going out with someone else wasn't funny to him.

••••••••●••••••••

Fall came too soon for Todd. He had worked hard during the summer to get in top shape; however, when football practice started, he realized how far behind he had gotten. Missing a year of playing this physical game meant that he had more ground to make-up than he realized.

He had been red-shirted his freshman year, which meant that he would be able to get an extra year of college and playing football.

His second year, he had to work extremely hard just to make the traveling squad. He was the fourth quarterback on the roster and saw very little action during the season. During practice, he did have to quarterback the scout team all season, which meant he took a beating every time they had to scrimmage the first team defense.

Denise made all of the home games, only to watch Todd pace the sideline. She knew that not playing bothered Todd more than he would admit to her.

Todd began to develop into a good college quarterback in the spring. During spring training, Todd worked out after practice every day to get the coach's attention. He was in the field house every time a coach was there. In the annual game ending spring practice, he was able to score a touchdown and throw a pass for another one. He had moved up to become the second team quarterback by the end of spring workouts.

Late in the spring semester, Denise was studying extra hard to continue her good grades. One night, while she was at the library, a nice looking fraternity guy came to her and said, "Hi! I'm Dan Tucker. What's your name?"

Startled, Denise looked up and said, "Hi. I'm Denise."

Dan replied, "Denise, I've been watching you and noticed you have been working extremely hard. Why don't you take a break and let me take you to get something to drink?"

She responded, "I'm sorry, but I must finish this."

"I'll wait for you to finish."

"You don't understand; I'm probably going to be here for a while."

"Then, I'll just have to wait longer."

"I'm sorry, but I can't!"

"Sure you can!"

Denise, getting frustrated with him, decided to be straight forward. She told him, "Dan, I'm sorry, but I'm dating someone."

Dan replied, "Where is he?"

"He plays football at Texas Eastern."

"Since he's not here, I'll just wait and make sure you get to the dorm safely."

Dan waited until Denise was through studying and talked to her as she walked to her dorm. He told her, "You really should let me get to know you better."

"I'm sorry, but the answer is still no!"

When she got to the dorm, he said, "Well, I guess I lost tonight, but I'll call you tomorrow."

"It won't do you any good!"

"Sooner or later, you'll get to know me. You never can tell, you might like me!"

When Denise got in her room, she told her roommate, Rachel, "Boy! Was that guy forward?"

Rachel asked, "What guy?"

"Dan Tucker! He wouldn't take no for an answer."

"Why did you have to say no?"

"He kept trying to persuade me to go get something to drink with him. Now he says he's going to call me tomorrow; however, he didn't get my last name. Maybe that'll put an end to that problem."

Rachel answered the telephone after the first ring, "Hello! It's for you!"

Denise, thinking it was Todd, answered, "Hello!"

Dan replied, "Denise, are you sure you don't want to go get something to drink?"

"How did you get my number?"

"I have my sources."

"The answer is still no, and don't call me again!"

"I'll continue to ask you until you accept."

"The answer will continue to be no. Goodbye!"

Rachel asked, "You really don't know who he is?"

"No, and I don't care to know!"

"Is he nice looking?"

"Sorta."

"Maybe you could introduce him to me!"

"That'll be fine with me. I'm going to bed."

The next day as Denise was getting ready to go to supper, the phone rang. Again, it was Dan. He said to her, "Denise this is Dan Tucker. Could I come by to see you?"

"Dan, why can't you understand I'm dating someone else and *will not* go out with you?"

"Could I talk to you face to face for just a few minutes? If you still don't want to go out with me, then I'll leave you alone."

"Okay, I guess so. I'll talk to you for just a few minutes, but you must understand I'm dating someone else and will not date you. That's final!"

"Fair enough! I'll be in the lobby in ten minutes."

When Dan saw Denise, he immediately approached her and said, "I'm glad you came down. Why don't we talk about this over supper? Let me take you to a nice restaurant off campus. It'll beat this dorm food."

Denise told him, "Dan, I want you to stop calling me. I'm not going anywhere with you. You might as well leave now."

Dan paused before he continued, "I don't take no for an answer very often. However, I'll honor your request. You're a very attractive girl. I may call you again, just in case you might break-up with your boyfriend."

Denise replied, "Thank you!" She turned and left for the cafeteria without looking back.

Rachel was just leaving the room, when the telephone rang. She picked up the receiver and said, "Hello!"

Todd asked, "Could I speak to Denise."

Being in a hurry, Rachel didn't recognize Todd's voice. She commented, "You'll have to wait in line. She's talking to Dan."

Todd replied, "Oh...uh...would you have her call me when she gets back."

Rachel snapped, "Sure! Who's this?"

"Just have her call Todd."

Rachel suddenly realized she had just made a big mistake and stuttered, "Uh...sure! Uh, just as soon as she gets back!"

After she put the receiver down, she rushed to the cafeteria to find Denise. She said to herself, "Was that a stupid mistake, or what? Why didn't I recognize his voice? I better find Denise, fast!"

When she saw her roommate eating, Rachel rushed up to her and said, "Denise! I just messed up. Todd called and I told him you were talking to Dan! I'm sorry! I guess I was in a hurry and didn't pay any attention to who was calling."

Denise told her, "I'm almost through. I'll go call him right now."

Todd turned to his roommate, Clay, and said, "That's great! Denise is talking to some guy named Dan."

Clay, remembering what happened the time Todd had seen Darren at Denise's house, joked, "You going to get drunk?"

Todd quickly looked back, paused, and stared at the snickering Clay. He commented, "No! I'm not getting drunk, at least until I hear Denise's side of the story."

"Good! Let's go eat!"

"You go ahead. I'm not going anywhere until she calls back."

Clay responded, "Then, I'll just stay here with you. How long do you think we'll have to wait?"

"I don't know, but I'm not leaving until she calls. You go on and eat!"

"No way! The last time you almost killed yourself!"

"Go ahead! I'm not going to lose my head this time."

"I'm waiting here until you're ready to eat!"

"Okay, but it may be a while!"

Shortly, the phone sounded. Todd answered it on the first ring, "Hello!"

Denise said, "Todd, that you?"

"Yes! Who were you talking to?"

"It was somebody who came up to me last night while I was studying at the library. He has been determined to take me out. He doesn't take no for an answer."

"Do I need to come over? I bet I can make him understand!"

"That won't be necessary! I finally made him understand that I wasn't going anywhere with him. He had to take the hint sooner or later."

"I'm going to eat and come over to see you!"

"No, Todd! Why don't you wait until tomorrow? It'll be Friday, and we can go to a movie or something. I promise you, I'm not going anywhere with this guy."

Todd hesitated, then reluctantly said, "Okay. Are you sure you don't need me to come over?"

"Yes, I'm positive! I'm studying for a math test I have to take tomorrow. I'll just stay in my room tonight."

"Okay, I'll pick you up at five o'clock tomorrow afternoon."

"Bye, Todd. I love you."

"I love you, too. Bye."

After Todd put the phone on the hook, Clay asked, "Everything okay?"

"Yeah! Some guy is trying to get her to go out with him. If he continues, I guess I'll have to introduce myself to him."

"I'm going with you when you go!"

"Let's eat!"

While Clay and Todd were eating, Clay could tell his roommate was still upset, so he asked, "Wanna talk about it?"

"Clay, Denise is very good looking. I've been expecting something like this to happen. What can I do to prevent it from happening again?"

Clay paused before telling Todd, "You could always get married!"

Todd didn't react to Clay's statement for a moment. Finally, he commented, "You know, I've been thinking about that for some time now. I don't like being separated from her." He paused a moment then continued, "We're still in college, and will be for a while! In fact, it may be a long time before we'll be able to get married."

Clay added, "Denise will be a senior at the end of the summer, or in December, at the latest."

Todd mentioned, "She would have to commute for over a year if we got married."

"Or she could transfer to Texas Eastern."

"That's true. However, I don't see her leaving SMU."

"Okay, but if you got married, you wouldn't have to worry about her going out with others."

Todd turned serious before he asked, "What would I do first?"

Clay thought a moment, then replied, "Why don't you call Coach Berry!"

"Hey, that's a great idea!"

After getting back to the dorm, Todd immediately called his former coach. When Bill Berry answered, Todd commented, "Coach, you've always said I could call on you if I had a problem. Right?"

"That's right. What's wrong?"

"Coach,...I...uh...I want to ask Denise to marry me. What should I do first?"

Coach Berry was surprised, but the news didn't shock him, either. He said, "Well, congratulations, Todd! I think the proper thing to do first would be to get permission from her father. When do you plan to propose?"

"Tomorrow night. I thought I'd take her to Reunion Tower and ask her there."

"That's pretty quick, isn't it?"

"Yes sir, it is!"

"Have you selected a ring?"

"No sir. Denise has always said she wanted to help choose her own ring."

Todd talked to his former coach for several minutes, getting ideas and suggestions about the proposal.

When he had finished his conversation, he got ready to call Mr. Poole. As he played with the numbers on the telephone, it seemed as though his fingers wouldn't work properly. It was exceptionally hard to make that call.

Clay, watching his roommate, started to laugh at Todd. Finally, he asked, "Something wrong, bud?"

Todd did not smile as he said, "This isn't as easy as I thought it would be. How do you ask someone if you can marry his daughter?"

Clay, trying not to laugh, replied, "Can't answer that question. I've never asked anyone before. You want me to dial Mr. Poole for you?"

"No! I'll do it myself! Clay, why don't you go somewhere else for a few minutes and let me do this myself?"

"Okay, but I think it would be more fun to stay here!"

Clay reluctantly left as Todd began to dial the Poole's residence. Todd thought, "If I'm lucky, maybe they won't be home tonight."

When Bettie Poole answered the phone, Todd stuttered, "Uh... Hello! Uh...is Mr....uh...Poole home?"

Bettie answered, "Sure, just a moment." As she handed the phone to her husband, she said, "It's Todd!"

Don Poole said, "Hello!"

Todd was extremely uneasy as he asked, "Uh…Mr. Poole, is that you?"

Mr. Poole smiled and answered, "Yes, it is! Is something wrong?"

"Uh, no sir, Mr. Poole. I need to ask you something, sir."

Don Poole noticed how nervous Todd sounded and began to realize what Todd was about to ask. Then, he started to get anxious. He asked Todd, "What can I do for you?"

"Mr. Poole, I would like to have your permission to marry Denise, sir." Todd could almost hear the silence on the other end of the phone.

Finally, he heard Mr. Poole say, "Bettie! Come here a moment!" As Bettie approached the phone, Don continued, "This is Todd. He's asking for permission to marry Denise."

Bettie asked, "Does Denise know about it?"

Todd answered the question before Don could relay the message, "No sir! I'm planning to ask her tomorrow night."

Mr. Poole, sounding more serious than Todd could ever remember, asked, "Do you love her?"

"Yes sir! Very much, sir!"

Todd was almost like one of the family already, but this was a very big step, and Don Poole wanted Todd to understand the seriousness of marriage.

The anxious father continued, "Denise is our only daughter, and she is very special to us. Do you want to spend the rest of your life with her?"

"Yes sir! I sure do, sir!"

"I expect you to always respect her and to treat her as something very special."

"Yes sir! I will, sir!"

"I know you will, and you have our blessings."

Tears began to fill Bettie's eyes as her husband hung up the phone. Don added, "I've been expecting this, but I had hoped they would finish school first."

"Me too, but you know they do love each other."

When Todd placed the receiver on the hook, he stood staring at the phone. He wondered how many times he had used the word "sir" in the conversation with Mr. Poole. His mind was racing, as was his heartbeat. He thought to himself, "Well Todd, it's too late to back out now!"

He didn't know what to do next. He sat in a chair and took a deep breath. Todd looked at his hands; they were still shaking. It was hard for him to comprehend what he had just done. He had just asked Mr. Poole if he could marry Denise.

He slowly went to the door to get Clay. He walked nervously to the lobby where his roommate was watching television. Todd called, "Clay!"

Clay jumped and followed Todd back to the room. By now, Clay was almost as tense as Todd. When Todd closed the door, Clay said, "Well! Tell me about it! How did it go?"

Todd, becoming fidgety, commented, "Clay, I'm about to propose to Denise. Do you know what that means?"

"Yeah, bud! You're about to get married!"

Todd sat in a chair and exclaimed, "Man! Do you think I'm ready for this?"

Clay became unusually serious when he stated, "Todd, you two have been in love for over two years now. You have the money, and you're on a full scholarship. I think you both are ready and will be very happy."

"What if she's not ready, yet?"

"Todd, you two have talked about getting married several times. I personally think she is ready."

"Gosh! What am I getting myself into?"

"A very good, close family. That's what! Congratulations, bud!"

Todd exclaimed, "Clay, I've got a lot to do to make tomorrow night special. I am going to need some help!"

"I'm ready! Where do we start?"

While Todd waited on Denise, Dan entered the dorm lobby. Dan didn't see Denise as she came down the stairs and headed for Todd.

When Denise saw Dan at the front desk, a strange expression came over her face.

Todd noticed her when she spotted Dan, and asked, "Who's that?"

"Uh...that's Dan!"

The woman behind the counter pointed out Denise to Dan. He turned around and saw Denise and Todd together, and both were looking in his direction. He decided it was time to leave the dorm and started toward the door.

Todd called, "Dan! Wait a minute!"

Denise asked, "Todd! What are you going to do?"

As he moved towards Dan, Todd stated, "Nothing! Stay here!"

Todd walked up to Dan and whispered something in his ear. Dan looked surprised, grinned slightly, and whispered something to Todd. The two men shook hands, and Dan left the lobby.

When Todd returned to Denise, she asked, "What did you say to him?"

"Nothing!"

"You're lying! What did you say?"

"I'll tell you later."

Denise was totally puzzled by the events she had just witnessed, but was relieved that there had not been a confrontation.

When they got in Todd's red Mustang, Denise asked, "Where are we going tonight?"

Todd answered, "I've got reservations at a special place. You'll see in a few minutes."

Denise looked at Todd and said, "You sure are acting strange tonight. What's wrong?"

"Nothing! Nothing's wrong! Why?"

"You're just acting strange."

When they drove up to Reunion Tower, Denise asked, "We're eating here?"

"Yeah! I haven't taken you to a nice place lately; you liked it here the night we graduated."

When they got to the top of the tower, a waiter took them to a nice table that was away from most of the people eating in the restaurant. The view of downtown Dallas was breathtaking.

Denise remarked, "Todd, this is really nice."

"Thank you!"

As the young couple ate, Todd became more and more nervous. When they finished their meal, Denise asked, "Todd, what's with you tonight? You seem so serious."

Todd shook his head as if to downplay his nervousness. Shortly, the waiter brought a small cake and placed it in front of Denise. On top of the cake were the words, "Will you marry me?"

Denise's eyes opened a little wider as she read it again, "Will you marry me?" When tears formed in her eyes, Todd dropped to one knee, took her hand and said, "Denise, I love you and want you to be my wife. Will you marry me?"

They both rose as Denise put her arms around his neck and exclaimed, "Yes! Yes! I'll marry you!"

After kissing each other, Denise sat down, took out a tissue, and wiped her eyes. She commented, "I knew you were acting strange, but I never suspected this. Do Mother and Dad know?"

Todd answered, "Yes, I talked to them last night. Would you like to go look at rings, tonight?"

"Yes! Where should we go?"

Todd replied, "Coach Preston has given me a name and place at a mall. He knows the owner of a jewelry store and told me to use his name if we go there."

A smiling waiter approached and asked, "Anything else, sir?"

Todd replied, "No! That'll be all."

As they were leaving, the waiter told them, "Congratulations!"

The excited couple replied, "Thank you!"

After they got in the car, Denise asked, "I want to know what you told Dan at the dorm?"

Todd smiled and said, "I told him I was going to propose to you tonight, and from now on, you were off limits!"

"What did he tell you?"

He congratulated me and said that you were the only girl that he couldn't get to go out with him.

At the mall, Denise picked out a beautiful ring. She told Todd, "This is exactly the kind of ring I have always dreamed about."

Todd asked, "You want to go show your parents tonight?"

As she stared at her new engagement ring, she exclaimed, "Yes! Let's go show them now!"

Don and Bettie Poole were just going to bed when Todd and Denise drove up. Both of her parents were excited. They bragged on the ring and warmly congratulated the young couple. Bettie asked, "When do you plan to get married?"

Denise told her, "We discussed the middle of June. That would give me time to go to summer school the second semester."

"This June?"

"Yes ma'am!"

Bettie exclaimed, "That doesn't give us much time!"

The excited mother talked non-stop as she and her daughter went to another room to do some planning.

Don looked at Todd and said, "Well, there won't be any peace around here for a while. Come on, we need to have a talk!"

·········●·········

As the organist played, Todd moved to the right side of the altar, wearing his solid white tuxedo. With his dark tan and sandy hair, the six-foot-three inch groom looked startling.

Lined up behind him was his best man, Clay Comer. Behind Clay was another friend and teammate, Ryan Rose. The last one in line was former high school teammate, Stanley Wilson.

The bridesmaids came in one at a time. The first one to enter was Denise's roommate, Rachel Tanner, followed by Cindy Smith, a high school friend, and finally Denise's best friend, Mandi Stowe.

Don and Bettie Poole were sitting on the left side of the sanctuary, while on the groom's side, Todd had asked Coach Bill Berry and his wife Beth to sit with his aunts and uncles to represent his family.

The church was filled with people to watch this popular young couple exchange their vows. Several college classmates had come to the wedding, including some of the football players. Todd's coach, Len Preston, and his wife, Angela, also made the trip from Texas Eastern.

Todd and Denise hardly smiled during the ceremony until they turned to face each other. As Denise looked up into Todd's eyes, each smiled affectionately at their new partner.

When the minister asked for the ring, Clay searched his pockets as if he couldn't find it. Finally, he snapped his fingers, reached down, and pulled the ring from his sock. Everyone laughed when Clay handed it to Todd. The handsome groom looked at Clay as if to say, "Your time is coming!"

Both Denise and Todd nervously repeated their vows. Finally, the minister said to the couple, "I now pronounce you husband and wife. Todd, you may kiss your bride."

The audience grinned as Todd kissed his wife. After the kiss, the minister proclaimed, "I'm proud to introduce for the first time, Mr. and Mrs. Todd Perry."

CHAPTER 15

The November sky was cool and clear as Texas Eastern prepared to finish their football season. Both teams lined up in the opposite end zones to enter the playing field.

Todd was excited, but he also realized this would be the last time he would ever play football. He was completing his fifth and final season in a Texas Eastern uniform.

He had talked to several professional football teams, but he knew that he had practically no chance of playing pro ball.

In the broadcast booth, the announcer was introducing the players to his radio audience. When he came to Todd's name, he announced, "Starting at quarterback for the last time in a Texas Eastern uniform is Todd Perry. He will be getting a degree this spring in education and plans to coach. His wife, Denise, is expecting their first child sometime next week."

Denise sat in the stands with her parents, Don and Bettie Poole. With them were Todd's high school coach, Bill Berry, and his wife, Beth.

The two teams finally charged onto the playing field as both bands played their respective fight songs.

When Todd reached the sideline, as always, he would find Denise in the stands. From time to time during the course of the game, he would look at her. They had been married a year and a half, and Todd was more in love than he could ever remember.

As play progressed, it became apparent that it would be a close and hard-fought game. Todd had completed several passes, one for a touchdown, early in the second quarter. However, he had taken several hits and had been sacked twice. It seemed as though the game got tougher as they approached half-time.

At the half, the Texas Eastern coaches chewed on their offensive linemen and encouraged them to block more aggressively.

Clay, who played defensive end, was on the sideline when Todd was on the field. When he got his first chance during half-time to talk to Todd, he asked, "Bud, you okay?"

"Sure, why?"

"I looked at Denise the last time you were hit, and she looked concerned that her hubby was getting mauled."

Todd replied, "I'm okay!"

In the stands, Denise, sitting next to her mother, watched Todd when the teams came back onto the field for the second half. She thought, "This will be his last half of playing football."

She was almost glad to see his playing days come to an end. He loved to play football, but the early start to the season, the training, and the long practice sessions had been hard on both of them.

When Denise became pregnant in the spring, matters became even more complicated.

It was ironic that the football season would end about the same time the baby was due. People had told them the baby would change their lives more than anything else they had known.

She waved at Todd when he got to the sideline. It always made her feel good for him to look up at her.

Early in the third quarter, Texas Eastern started to move the football down the field. With the score tied 7 to 7, they needed a time consuming drive. On second and short yardage, Todd completed a fifteen yard pass across the middle, for a first down.

Everyone in the stands jumped up and cheered for the big gain and another first and ten. As Denise jumped up, a sharp pain hit her. She had witnessed some false labor pains over the past few days, but this one was much stronger. She immediately sat down. Her mother didn't notice any problem, because many of the fans started to sit back down at the end of the play.

As the pain eased, Denise relaxed. She didn't say anything to her mother, but if it happened again, she would have to tell her.

Her mother turned to Denise and commented, "That was a nice pass!"

Denise acknowledged, "Yes, it was!"

Several plays later, an even sharper pain hit her. This time, she grabbed her mother's arm. Bettie Poole quickly turned to her daughter and asked, "What's wrong, dear?"

"I just had another pain!"

"*Another* pain? How many have you had?"

"That's only the second one. I've been having some false labor pains, but these really hurt!"

Bettie turned to her husband and said, "Don! Denise has had some sharp pains! We need to get her out of the stands!"

"What kind of pains?"

Bettie whispered, "Labor pains!"

"What? Well, let's get her out of here!"

Denise said, "Wait a minute! Let's don't get in a hurry. It might not be anything to'em."

As the Texas Eastern offense moved into scoring range, another sharp pain caused Denise to double over. She exclaimed, "Oh! This one really hurts! Oh!"

Bettie looked at her astonished husband and said, "That's it! Let's get her to the first aid station!"

Coach Berry, sitting next to Mr. Poole, asked, "What's wrong?"

Don responded, "I think Denise may be going into labor!"

"What! How long has this been going on?"

"They just started! We're going to take her to the first aid station!"

Don Poole and Bill Berry held Denise's hands and helped her from the stands. Then they escorted her to the first aid station under the stadium as Bettie and Beth followed.

When the next pain hit her, Bettie stated, "That's it! It's time to take her to the hospital!"

Don commented, "We need to let Todd know!"

Denise exclaimed, "No! We can't! He couldn't do anything now but worry. Let him finish the game!"

Bettie asked, "Are you sure?"

"Yes ma'am! It'll be hours before the baby comes, even if this is real labor. Todd can come after the game!"

Don told Coach Berry, "You and Beth stay and tell Todd after the game! We're taking Denise to the hospital in Dallas!"

Coach Berry answered, "Okay! We'll see that he gets there as quickly as possible!"

Denise remarked, "Thank you, Coach!"

Don told Bettie, "You stay with her while I go get the car. I'll come to the gate out front."

A first aid attendant told them, "I'll get a wheelchair for her to use!"

Denise insisted, "I can walk!" Suddenly another sharp pain hit her and she gave in. "Maybe I had better use the wheelchair!"

When the anxious father and Coach Berry placed her in the car, Bill assured her, "Don't worry about Todd! We'll get him to the hospital just as soon as the game is over!"

Denise told him, "Make sure he showers. I don't want him coming to the hospital in his uniform!"

Everyone laughed as the coach assured her he would have her husband clean when he arrived

Late in the third quarter, the offense completed the long drive that had taken over seven minutes off the game clock. Todd scored on a quarterback keeper around right end that gave Texas Eastern a 14 to 7 lead.

With their solid defense led by defensive end Clay Comer and linebacker Ryan Rose, they now seemed to have control of the game.

When Todd reached the sideline, he noticed that Denise was not in her place. As Clay was preparing to go onto the field after the kickoff, Todd told him, "I'll be glad when that baby gets here. Denise spends half of her time going to the bathroom."

The two best friends watched the kickoff together. After the tackle, Clay checked with his coach to see what defense to use. He then ran to the defensive huddle and called the defense. As he buckled his chinstrap, he shouted the pass coverage to the secondary.

Halfway through the fourth quarter, Todd again looked for Denise. She was still not in her seat. Then he noticed that the Pooles and the Berrys were gone, also. He was beginning to wonder where they were when everyone on the Texas Eastern side began to yell.

Todd looked around as Coach Preston shouted, "Fumble! Hey Todd, let's finish them off! Hit 'em with a throwback pass. Maybe we can catch the off-side safety and corner sleeping!"

"Yes sir!"

Todd called for the throwback pass, broke the huddle, and sprinted to the line of scrimmage. Before the defense had time to get organized, Todd took the snap, sprinted to the left, planted his left foot, and spun back to the right. He fired a smooth spiral pass to a racing wide receiver. It was perfect. The defensive backs were unable to keep up with the streaking receiver, and could only watch as he crossed the goal line.

That was it! Texas Eastern was in a good position to win their final game of the season.

Todd came off the field as Coach Preston and the rest of the team congratulated him on a great play.

Clay commented, "Great pass, bud!"

Todd asked Clay, "Did you see Denise leave?"

"No! Why?"

"Well, the Pooles and the Berrys are also gone!"

"What does that mean?"

"I don't know. Sure hope everything's okay!"

Todd was through playing, when the back-up quarterback went into the game on the next offensive series.

Todd stood by Clay and told him, "Well, guess I'm through with college football."

"Yeah! Me too."

Uncharacteristically, they hugged each other. Todd admitted, "It's been good, Clay!"

"Sure has, bud!"

Todd looked back at Denise's empty seat. He was becoming uneasy. She had been gone since the middle of the third quarter. He thought, *"That's too long just to go to the restroom; besides, she wouldn't take the whole family with her."*

Finally, the game ended. The seniors congratulated each other and shook hands with their opponents.

Todd again looked for his wife. Suddenly, he heard Coach Berry's voice, "Todd! Hey, Todd!"

Todd turned to greet his former coach. Before he could say anything, Coach Berry explained, "Todd, you need to hurry! Denise has gone into labor!"

"What?"

"Denise went into labor right after half-time. Her parents have taken her to the hospital. Hurry-up! Beth and I are supposed to take you there!"

"Is she okay?"

"Everything was fine when they left the stadium!"

"That's a relief! I knew something wasn't right. Would you tell Coach Preston where I'm going?"

"Sure, but hurry!"

As Todd ran off the field, he turned and hollered to Coach Berry, "Tell Clay, too!"

When Todd finished taking a shower, he hurried to get dressed. He was buttoning his shirt as he started out of the dressing room. Clay was rushing in and almost ran over his best friend.

Clay immediately asked, "You heading to Dallas?"

"Yeah, Coach Berry's taking me!"

"Let me have the keys to your car, and Cindy and I will bring it over later. Good luck!"

"Thanks, Clay! I may need you before this is over!" They shook hands as Todd left.

Several of the players were beginning to drift into the dressing room as Todd was leaving. Coach Preston called, "Todd! Good luck, I'll come see you later!"

"Thanks, Coach!"

Beth had the car ready when the two men ran out of the field house. As they drove off, Coach Berry told Todd what had happened during the game.

Todd was anxious to see Denise when he entered the labor room. His sandy hair was combed, but still damp when he hugged his laboring wife. He asked, "You okay?"

As another pain hit her, she shouted, "No! This hurts!"

She was sweaty and clammy as she struggled with the pain.

Bettie Poole assured him, "The doctor said she is fine, but it may be a while before the baby comes."

After holding Denise's hand for a while, Todd began to get nervous. He remembered her broken leg and how much pain she had suffered then. Yet, this was different. This time, she was going to give birth to their first child.

He wished Denise didn't have to suffer so much. He prayed quietly, "Lord, you have taken care of us so many times. Please help Denise through this pain."

Todd had grown spiritually since he and Denise had been married, and they very seldom missed church. During this time of anxiety, he found himself turning to God for strength.

Todd and Bettie took turns staying with Denise, but as the pains got stronger and she began to get tired, Todd found it hard to leave her side.

Don Poole, along with Bill and Beth Berry, stayed in the waiting room. Clay and Cindy soon came in. Cindy immediately asked about Denise.

Clay listened to the latest news on the baby, but looked around for Todd. Don told them, "You two might as well sit down. Things are going rather slow at the moment."

Todd had told the Berrys they didn't have to stay, but they insisted on remaining in the waiting room.

Todd wondered how time could pass so slowly. He remembered how it had crept when Denise had surgery to set her broken leg, but this was even more disturbing. Not only was she getting tired, but she was getting weaker. She also was in a very foul mood. He couldn't seem to say anything to make her feel better.

The doctor and nurses wouldn't tell him much except, "The baby will come when it's ready." Todd had heard that several times, and it was getting old.

As he waited, he began to grow stiff from the contact he had received in the football game. He thought, *"I've just finished my last football game, and have hardly thought about it."*

He looked at his miserable wife and prayed that the baby would hurry up.

It was in the early morning hours when the doctor told the nurse, "Move her into the delivery room. I think it's about ready to make its entrance."

Since Todd was going to be with Denise during the delivery, he had to clean-up and put on surgical clothes. His heart began to speed up as he kissed Denise. He told her, "I'll be there shortly."

When a nurse led him into the delivery room, he had never seen Denise in such pain. It almost made him sick to see the one he loved go through this kind of agony.

All he could do was hold her hand, help her breath, and give her encouragement.

Things didn't seem to go any faster in the delivery room. Todd watched as Denise agonized. He kept saying to himself, "Hurry up! Hurry!" He prayed for Denise and the baby.

Finally, the doctor told her, "Push!"

Denise shouted back, "I am pushing!"

The doctor reassured her, "It won't be long now! Come on, push!"

Todd was beginning to feel faint. Things had begun to happen fast now. Everything began to turn white.

A nurse asked him, "Todd, you okay?"

He took a deep breath and said, "I think so!"

Denise let out a loud scream. The doctor exclaimed, "That's it! It's a big healthy boy, and I think he has a football in his hand!"

The baby was cleaned, wrapped in a small blanket, and laid in Denise's arms.

Todd couldn't believe it! His very own son. He thought to himself, *"How can anything so ugly and red look so beautiful?"*

He looked at Denise, who was crying and looking at her newborn son. Todd had never been this proud in his whole life. With all of the excitement he had witnessed in sports and falling in love with a beautiful woman, there was nothing to compare to this feeling. Surely, this was an act of God.

Todd took Denise's hand and proudly proclaimed, "This is the most beautiful picture I have ever seen...my wife holding my son."

Todd proudly hustled into the waiting room to tell everyone about his new son. Beth Berry asked, "What's his name?"

"Philip Todd Perry. We're going to call him Phil!"

Clay could hardly talk as he muttered, "Congratulations Dad! Is Denise alright?"

"Thanks Clay! Denise is tired and weak, but happy that it's over!" Todd paused and added, "Clay, I've never seen Denise as radiant as she was holding our son. She was simply beautiful."

Clay could tell that his best friend was a proud father.

Coach Preston had come to Dallas to check on Todd and Denise. He stayed until the baby was born. He congratulated his quarterback and told him he would check on all of them later. He asked if he could do anything at their apartment. Todd told him that he thought everything was okay.

After Coach Preston left, Clay asked Todd, "Could I take you to get something to eat or drink?"

"Thanks Clay, but I want to get back to Denise."

When Todd returned to the delivery room, two nurses were preparing to move Denise to her room. He told her about the excitement in the waiting room and how everyone reacted to the news of the birth of their son.

Denise was then moved to her room, while the baby was moved to the nursery.

Todd kissed Denise and took this chance to walk to the nursery.

From the hallway, he saw everyone staring through the nursery window. He thought, *"Man! He already has a cheering section!"*

When Todd arrived at the window, everyone stepped back so the new father could look at his son. Bettie Poole still had tears in her eyes, and her husband Don just stood at the window smiling.

Coach Berry told Todd, "Congratulations, Todd. I know you're proud. He's a nice looking, healthy boy. Beth and I are going to leave. Call me if you need anything."

"Thanks Coach, I appreciate you and Beth being here. It means a lot to me. I would have passed out cigars, but I guess you know I was caught by surprise."

They shook hands as the Berrys told everyone goodbye and left. Clay and Cindy were the next to leave. Todd noticed that Clay was more emotional than he had expected. He appreciated Clay being with him during the birth of his son. He had been a true friend.

Finally, it was only Todd and the proud grandparents staring at the newborn baby. Todd was tired and stiff. Today he had played a very physical football game and then witnessed his wife give birth to his son. However, in spite of all of this exhausting activity, he had a hard time remembering when he had felt so good.

Around mid-morning the next day, Denise and Todd were waiting for a nurse to bring the baby to its mother. The door opened and the nurse brought the bundled baby and placed it in Denise's arms.

It was a picture of beauty for Todd. When the nurse left, Denise told him, "Here, you hold him."

Todd couldn't move. He stuttered, "But he...he's...so tiny."

"Here, you have to hold him sometimes!"

"Okay, just a second."

Todd removed his billfold from his back pocket and pulled out a picture of his parents. He placed it upright on a table. He took his son from Denise, cradled him in his arms, and looked at the picture.

"Mom, Dad…I want you to meet your new grandson, Phil."

That evening, as the proud father was driving home, he noticed the gibbous moon. It no longer appeared to be a football, but looked like a large tear drop in the night sky. Todd now believed Sherry and Philip Todd Perry knew they were grandparents.

www.ingramcontent.com/pod-product-compliance
Ingram Content Group UK Ltd.
Pitfield, Milton Keynes, MK11 3LW, UK
UKHW022227230426
12048UKWH00016BA/1117